A Gangsta's Code 2:
Thug Immortal

Lock Down Publications and
Ca$h Presents

A Gangster's Code

A Novel by **J-Blunt**

A Gangster's Code 2

Lock Down Publications
P.O. Box 870494
Mesquite, Tx 75187

Visit our website
www.lockdownpublications.com

Lock Down Publications
Like our page on Facebook: Lock Down Publications @
www.facebook.com/lockdownpublications.ldp
Cover design and layout by: **Dynasty Cover Me**
Book interior design by: **Shawn Walker**
Edited by: **Lauren Burton**

Stay Connected with Us!

Text **LOCKDOWN** to 22828 to stay up-to-date with new releases, sneak peeks, contests and more…

A Gangster's Code 2

Submission Guideline.

Submit the first three chapters of your completed manuscript to ldpsubmissions@gmail.com, subject line: Your book's title. The manuscript must be in a .doc file and sent as an attachment. The document should be in Times New Roman, double-spaced and in size 12 font. Also, provide your synopsis and full contact information. If sending multiple submissions, they must each be in a separate email.

Have a story but no way to send it electronically? You can still submit to LDP/Ca$h Presents. Send in the first three chapters, written or typed, of your completed manuscript to:

LDP: Submissions Dept
Po Box 870494
Mesquite, Tx 75187

DO NOT send original manuscript. Must be a duplicate.

Provide your synopsis and a cover letter containing your full contact information.

Thanks for considering LDP and Ca$h Presents.

J-Blunt

Prologue

10 years earlier

Three masked men blended in with the night as they moved swiftly from the bushes to the back door. The lick was a safehouse. As told to the robbers, behind the door was the key to their futures: over $100,000 in cash and 25 kilos of Columbian cocaine. The only thing that lay between them and their prize was a locked door and a fool with loose lips. Born Ready had been in the house twice and knew the layout. They would enter through the back door into the kitchen. A hallway to the left would take them to the bedroom. The safe was built into the floor, literally hidden beneath the floorboards, welded in place. The vic would have to open it. That was the only way to get the contents inside. One thing in their favor was the house didn't have the best security system, just an alarm that only got used when the owner was out. Since he didn't think anyone was bold enough to hit the house while he was in it, M-Dot never turned on the alarm while he was home. Never.

Born Ready looked to his accomplices, locking eyes with each one. When he was sure they were on the same page, he lifted a hand, using his fingers to count to three.

The masked men crashed into the door at the same time. Locks snapped and wood splintered as the door caved in. Born Ready led the way, his 9 mm Ruger cocked and ready.

The loud crash at the back door jarred M-Dot from his sleep. Without being fully awake, he knew what was happening, and instincts kicked in. He shot out of bed, going for the AK-47 underneath the mattress. For fear of the gun going off while he was fucking or sleeping, the chopper was never loaded, but there was a 30-round clip right next to it. He had just locked it in place and was about to load a bullet into the chamber.

"Put it down, bitch," Born Ready screamed, the red dot of his beam centering on M-Dot's chest.

M-Dot was a big man, 6'2", 280 pounds, but he wasn't big enough to stop a bullet. The assault rifle fell to the floor and M-Dot put his hands in the air.

"You know what it is, nigga!" one of Born Ready's accomplices spoke up. His name was Mecca. "Open dat safe, fuck-boy! Give dat shit up!"

"I-I d-don't know what chu talkin' 'bout, mane," M-Dot stuttered, studying the robbers for a sign of something familiar. It was hard because they were dressed in black and wore masks.

"That ain't cho shit, brah," Born Ready spoke up. "We know this Kareem shit. And we know where the safe at. Pull up the rug and open it."

"C'mon, brah. I don't know what you talkin' 'bout. Ain't no safe up in here."

Born Ready was a few inches shorter than M-Dot and a hundred pounds lighter, but he attacked the bigger man like the roles had been reversed. A couple 9 mm slaps to the face felled the bigger man. "Open that safe, nigga! Give dat shit up!"

M-Dot balled up on the floor and began screaming. "I don't know what chu talkin 'bout!"

"Pull that rug up," Born Ready ordered his third accomplice.

Reese was Born Ready's little big brother. At 17, he was 6'3", 175 pounds and still growing. The gangly teen pulled up the colorful throw rug, exposing polished hardwood floors. While Born Ready held M-Dot at gunpoint, Mecca and Reese lifted the removable floorboards, exposing a 4' x 4' safe.

"Oh shit! Look at this, M-Dot. A safe in yo' muthafuckin' floor," Born Ready patronized.

A Gangster's Code 2

A welt had formed on M-Dot's jaw, and another above his eye. He uncurled from the fetal position long enough to look around. The safe was exposed and the robbers stood around watching his next move. That's when a noise sounded from somewhere in the house, like someone was moving around.

"Watch 'im," Born Ready told Mecca, who pulled a .45 from his waist.

The brothers crept through the house searching for who or what had made the noise. There was another bedroom at the end of the hall that turned out to be empty. There was another door across the hall. When Born Ready tried the knob, it was locked. After taking a step back, he kicked the door open.

"Ah!" a woman screamed.

The goons rushed into the bathroom and found a scantily clad woman trying to pry open a bathroom window that had been painted shut. Born Ready pointed is pistol at her, flashing the beam to get her attention. "Chill. Don't scream no more or I'ma pop yo' ass. Who is you?"

"I-I'm M-Myra," she stuttered, wrapping her arms across her chest to cover her heaving bosom. Dressed in a pair of purple panties and bra, the brothers seen enough to agree M-Dot had good taste in women. She had honey-colored skin, shoulder-length permed hair, big breasts, thick thighs and an ass that made Reese's young body lose control.

"Who is you to M-Dot?" Born Ready asked.

"I-I'm his fiancée."

A light went on in Born Ready's eyes. "How long y'all been together?"

"Almost five years. P-Please don't hurt me. I don't got nothin' to do wit' whatever he do in the streets."

"Don't worry, baby. Long as M-Dot give us what we want, ain't nobody gon' get hurt. C'mon back to the room so we can talk."

Myra, Reese, and Born Ready went back to the room and found M-Dot still on the floor, Mecca watching him at gunpoint. When he seen the honey-skinned beauty, he looked her over. "Who is she?" Mecca asked.

"Myra. M-Dot's fiancée," Born Ready smiled. "She gon' make him open the safe."

"Please, baby. Just give 'em what they want," the woman pleaded.

"Nah, baby," he refused. "Either they gon' kill us after they take it or Kareem gon' kill us if they take it."

Mecca lost his patience and put the 45 to M-Dot's head. "Listen, nigga! I ain't got time for this shit. Open the safe!"

M-Dot feared for his life, but not enough to open the safe. "I can't do it, brah. Just kill me."

Mecca pointed the gun at Myra. "Open that safe or yo' bitch dead."

M-Dot looked like he wanted to cry. "C'mon, brah. Just let her go. Let her leave right now and I'ma open the safe. I swear to God."

Mecca looked to Born Ready, waiting for an answer.

"Nah, it don't work like that. We make the rules. Matter fact, you see how my li'l brotha lookin' at cho bitch? She don't want him to pull them pants down. Shit gon' get real ugly. Unless you want yo' bitch to piss out her ass for the rest her life, open that safe," Born Ready said.

Mecca, Myra and M-Dot looked from Born Ready to the long and lean teen. His eyes were locked on the woman's body parts like a dog watching food. A noticeable lump was growing in the front of his pants.

"Awe, c'mon, brah. We ain't on no rape shit," Mecca spoke up, looking disgusted.

Born Ready mugged his friend. "Fuck what chu talkin' 'bout. We doin' what we gotta do to get this money."

"Please, y'all. Don't do this," Myra begged.

"It ain't us. Tell that nigga to give us the money."

A Gangster's Code 2

Myra cried crocodile tears as she faced her fiancé. "Please, baby. Don't let them do this to me. Give 'em the money."

M-Dot's eyes watered as he felt his girl's fear, but that wasn't enough to make him open the safe, so Born Ready gave his little brother a head nod.

When Reese released his pants, his dick shot out like a missile. Nothing about the boy's manhood was average. It was deformed, crooked, with lumps as big as knuckles on the shaft. And it was massive, more than a foot long and wide as a baseball bat.

Mecca looked horrified. "What the fuck is that?"

The fear of God was written on Myra's face as she backed away from Reese like he was about to attack her with a weapon. "No! No! No! Don't come by me! Get it away from me!"

"Get her!" Born Ready encouraged.

The teen lunged for the woman and a struggle ensued. Myra, in fear for her life, had super strength the boy was no match for. She easily overpowered him, forcing Born Ready to help his little brother. After they pinned her down, Reese was able to snatch her panties off. After more struggling, they were able to pry her legs open. That's when Myra began scratching and screaming.

"Stop! Stop! Let me go!"

Born Ready's pistol across her face made her stop screaming. Reese was about to force his monstrosity inside her when M-Dot caved. "Okay! Okay, mane!"

All eyes flocked to the wounded fiancé.

"Okay, mane. Leave her alone. Take this shit. Tell that nigga to put that shit up."

Born Ready looked at Reese. "We good, brah."

Reese reluctantly crawled from the bed, disappointment and lust swirling in his eyes.

J-Blunt

When the safe was opened, Born Ready gave Reese the pistol to keep an eye on their prisoners while they filled pillowcases with drugs and money. In total they collected $150,000 and 30 kilos. After tying up the terrified lovers, the bandits made for the back door.

They had just stepped outside when a bright searchlight shone, cutting through the darkness like a laser beam.

***

When the call came over the radio for a possible home invasion in progress, Officer Daniels glanced at his young partner, the thrill of action spreading across his clean-shaven face. "That's a few blocks away, new booty. Radio in and tell 'em we're on our way."

The brown-skinned cadet didn't share his training officer's excitement for action. His hand visibly trembled as he grabbed the radio from the dash. "Squad 212 is in the area. Will radio when on scene. Out."

It took the squad car less than a minute to get on scene. Officer Daniels steered down the block at a slow pace, his eyes darting back and forth, looking for signs of trouble. When he was satisfied all was clear, he turned into the alley, flashing the spotlight on what looked like a broken door. In that same instant, three masked men ran outside. Two of them were carrying white sacks and were armed.

"Freeze! Police!" the rookie yelled, drawing his weapon as he jumped from the car.

When Reese heard the voice and seen the spotlight, his instincts took over and he began shooting. The rookie took cover behind the car door, firing four shots in retaliation. Two of them hit Reese, one in the leg, the other in the stomach. During the commotion, Mecca let off a few shots, hitting the rookie in the ankle before he ran away. Born Ready had taken a few steps toward freedom when he seen his little brother go down. Anger and guilt hit him in the same instant,

12

causing him to pause. The indecision gave the training officer the time he needed to get out of the car and take aim. Six pops sounded. Three bullets to the chest and stomach put the older brother on the ground next to his sibling. Mecca never broke stride, fleeing with a pillowcase full of goodies.

J-Blunt

Chapter 1

Present Day

Three black Suburbans coasted along the highway in a small envoy, ninety percent tint making it hard to see who was inside. All the trucks held heavily armed men, but there was something special about the middle truck. Five people were inside: two in the driver and passenger seats, one in the middle row, and two more in the back seats. Everyone in the truck was Mexican except the man in the middle seat. He was big, 6'4", 260 pounds and a muscular physique. His skin was dark as chocolate, combined with shoulder-length dreadlocks, and a full beard. The brown-skinned men in the back row whispered in Spanish about the stranger's bloody clothes and the blood-soaked package in his hands. Even though Pop Somethin' was unarmed and at their mercy, the cartel members were uncomfortable in the bigger man's presence, as they should have been. Their passenger was a real life boogeyman and legend.

The convoy of trucks drove into a small airport, parking in one of the hangars. Twenty members of the Gonzalez Cartel stood around a Lear Jet, armed to the teeth with machine guns.

"Let's go, Shooter," called the man in the passenger seat as he exited the truck. His name was Marco, a high-ranking bodyguard in the cartel. He stood average height with a slim build and short, dark hair. A white dress shirt, fitted denim jeans, and cowboy boots gave him a conservative look. In one hand he held a .44 Magnum. In the other was Pop Somethin's machete.

"You owe me an apology for disrespectin' me," Pop Somethin' told Marco as he stepped from the SUV.

"I don't apologize to dead people," Marco sneered, gesturing toward the million-dollar jet.

"You will," the killer promised.

Marco and two gunmen escorted Pop Somethin' to the plane. When he stepped into the cabin, Gonzo let out a snort. The Cartel boss was seated in a reclining chair, dressed similarly to Marco. A cowboy hat, black dress shirt, dark jeans, and hand-sown shoes. He stroked his thick mustache, looking Pop Somethin' from head to toe. "Looks like you been busy," he commented, noticing the bloody package.

"I didn't snitch on you, boss. I ain't wit' that fuck-shit. I believe in codes and laws in the streets. I ain't no bitch or snitch."

Gonzo studied Pop Somethin' for a few moments, searching for a sign of deceit or fakeness. Pop stared back, his posture and facial expression matching his words.

"What is that?" Gonzo asked, nodding toward the bloody package.

Pop Somethin' unwrapped the package, palming the severed head in his massive hand. "I brought C-Note."

Gonzo's eyes bulged and he looked at Marco, questioning him silently.

"He wouldn't let us touch it. Wouldn't even tell us what it was. Said it was for you."

"Get rid of it," he told Marco. "Shooter, have a seat."

A small table separated Gonzo and Pop Somethin'. On it was a bottle of tequila and half a kilo of cocaine.

"Tequila?" the boss offered.

Pop declined. "I'm good on the drink."

Gonzo poured two shots and pushed one in front of Pop Somethin'. "In Mexico, when someone offers you something, even if you don't want it, you must accept. To deny an offering is a sign of disrespect. Drink up. I insist."

Pop eyed Gonzo as he took the glass and downed the shot. When he slammed the glass on the table, Gonzo filled it again. Pop gave him a sideways look. Gonzo nodded. After a irritated deep breath, Pop took another drink. When he sat the shot glass down, Gonzo filled it again. He kept at it until Pop had downed fifteen shots. Since he didn't drink, the liquor took effect quickly. The jet's cabin began swirling and tilting as Pop's equilibrium tilted.

"How do you feel, Shooter?" Gonzo asked, his thick mustache lifting at the corners as he smiled.

"I'm fucked up," Pop slurred, his head lolling from side-to-side as his vision doubled.

"Good. That's how I feel. Fucked up. *Federales* up my ass. I lose millions of dollars and thousands of kilos. My farm in *Tijuana* is gone. I thought you and Note *mi amigos.* I took you in despite what my people say and how I feel about blacks. I know you didn't snitch, Shooter. I recognize what you are. But you and the headless guy were a team. A package. You came together. When I have a problem, I erase the whole thing and start over. Why should this time be different?"

"'Cause I ain't no bitch or snitch," Pop slurred. "Gonzo, you my nigga, boss. You showed me shit I never seen. Took me places I never been. When I look in yo' eyes, I see realness. Same shit you see when you look in mine. That's why I cut that nigga head off. Principles. Judgment. Consequences. Pussy niggas don't deserve to breathe the same air as me. He was havin' a baby by my cousin. I hated to bring my cousin pain, but fuck niggas s'posed to get fucked. I ain't no fuck nigga, Gonzo. Cut me and I bleed real nigga red. I don't give a fuck who they is, niggas break the rules and they gotta die. I ain't break no rules. I enforce 'em. You can't kill me, boss. I can't die. It ain't my time. I know you hold the power of life and death in yo' hands, but not mine. The world need more niggas like me. Like us."

Pop Somethin's head dropped forward after he finished speaking. Gonzo smirked, downing a shot of tequila

"You gonna let him talk to you like that, boss?" Marco spoke. "He's a rat, just like his nigger friend. Kill–"

Marco stopped speaking when Gonzo lifted a hand. "You must learn not to disrespect another man's race or culture. What you said to Shooter was wrong and unnecessary. The reason I allowed him on my plane and accept him getting blood on my seats is because we are equals. He doesn't have the money or stature, but we share principles. What I learned on the streets in Mexico, he learned in the streets of Texas. I bleed the same realness. You owe him an apology."

Marco's jaw slackened and a confused look spread across his face. "He a rat. I don't owe him anything but a bullet."

"You let me worry about who owes what. For now, you owe him. Pay. Apologize."

Pop looked up with a drunken grin on his face. Marco mugged him. "*Lo siento*," he apologized through tight lips that uttered insincere words.

Pop laughed. "Fuck you very much."

Marco's face turned red as he tightened his grip on the .44 and machete. "You're a dead man walking, Shooter. Dead!"

Pop Somethin' tried to stand, but lost his balance, falling back into the seat.

"Whoa, big man!" Gonzo laughed.

It took Pop Somethin' two more attempts before he was able to get to his feet, then he turned to Marco, swaying like a tree blowing in the wind. "I know you disrespect me 'cause you envy me. You see the way bitches look at me. Shit got chu mad 'cause they know my dick bigger than yours," Pop laughed. "The boss respect me 'cause I'm his equal. I knew him for a couple months and he see me as his peer. You knew him yo' whole life and you still a worker. Am I shinin' too bright? Is my light hurtin' yo' eyes?"

Marco attempted a lunge, but Gonzo's voice stopped him mid-stride. "Not on my plane! If you insist on a dick-measuring contest, take it outside. But Shooter, I warn you. You are in no condition to take on Marco. Even sober, he would be a hard match. He is the head of my security for a reason."

Pop Somethin' roared a laugh. "God ain't made a nigga that can fuck in my bidness."

All of the men from the Gonzalez Cartel formed a circle around the combatants. Pop Somethin' swayed from side-to-side, the liquor taking more and more of his bearing with every passing minute. Across from him, Marco shadow-boxed and kicked the air, showing his Jujitsu training.

"Are you sure about this, Shooter?" Gonzo asked, wearing a concerned look.

Pop gave another drunken smile and threw up his hands. Marco moved with the speed and experience of a trained fighter and was inside Pop's guard before the big man could react. Three punches to the face and a leg kick made Pop's knee buckle. When the spinning back-fist connected to his jaw, the fight appeared to be over. The big man stumbled backward, dazed, damaged, and woozy. But he didn't fall.

Marco knew he had struck damaging blows and the fight was over. He smiled victoriously, approaching Pop Somethin' with his hands down, swaggering like he'd already won. "This will be a fight to the death. I want to feel the life drain from your body. Then I will take your head and mount it on my wall next to your snitch bitch."

Pop Somethin' struggled to keep his balance, his head swirling from the liquor and punches. When Marco came close, Pop took a wild swing. The martial arts student ducked the wild blow and kicked Pop Somethin' in the knee again. When the big man stumbled, Marco took two steps and jumped in the air, his fist high behind his head. The Superman punch crashed into Pop's bearded jaw, rattling his teeth and cutting the inside of his cheek. The goon wobbled, swayed, and teetered, but he didn't fall. Blood leaked from

J-Blunt

his lips and pooled in his mouth. He spit a fountain of blood
before wiping his mouth and putting his dukes up again.

"You are a tough son of a bitch, I'll give you that,"
Marco admitted. "But you will go down. The bigger they are,
the harder they fall."

Pop rolled his shoulders and tried to shake the stars from
his head. He knew he was fucked up, but he couldn't feel the
pain.

In an attempt to put Pop out of his misery, Marco moved
quickly, stepping inside of Pop's guard before he could
throw a punch. The smaller man landed several punches to
Pop's face, his speed too much for the drunken man to elude.
Another kick to his tender leg made Pop's knee buckle.
When Marco twisted his body in an attempt to land a perfectly executed, full crescent roundhouse kick, Pop Somethin'
caught his leg. Marco tried to pull away, but his speed and
fighting skill was no match for Pop Somethin's strength. A
hard twist of his leg made Marco scream in pain as his knee
popped. He fell to the ground, trying to wiggle away, but
Pop didn't let go of his leg. He twisted again, tearing muscles, ligaments, and sinew. More screams filled the airplane
hangar. Other soldiers made a move to help, but a grunt from
Gonzo made them pause.

Everyone watched as the drunken, bloody, and dreadlocked black man picked Marco up from the ground, lifting
him over his head. With all the force he could muster, Pop
Somethin' brought the smaller man crashing down onto his
knee, almost breaking him in half. Bones crunched as
Marco's spine shattered across Pop's knee. Screams of ago-
ny filled the hangar as Marco's limp body fell to the ground.
Some of the cartel members looked away, disgusted by the
unnatural folding of their once-esteemed leader's body. A
beastly growl from Pop Somethin' made them all look to the
gruesome scene again. The sight would haunt their dreams
for several lifetimes.

20

A Gangster's Code 2

Pop Somethin' crawled on top of Marco, turning into a vampire as he used his teeth to rip out the paralyzed man's Adam's apple and voice box. Blood sprayed from Marco's throat like a geyser as Pop snatched his head back, his face covered in fresh blood as he chewed the dying man's throat. After spitting out the mangled flesh, Pop knelt next to Marco and watched him die.

"What a waste," Gonzo said disgustedly, turning to his militia. "Let this be a lesson to you all. Enemies must die or they will recover from small wounds. But they can never re-cover from a great death."

After taking a few moments to let his words sink in, the cartel boss turned to Pop Somethin'. "You have 72 hours to leave Texas. My reach knows no boundaries. This is your only warning. Do not come back."

J-Blunt

Chapter 2

Tires squealed and gravel flew in the air as the Maserati sped past the chain-link fence that separated the outside world from the small airport. The woman behind the wheel of the sports car wore a panicked look. Her identical twin in the passenger seat wore the same expression.

"Find hangar nineteen!" Queenie said, her eyes wide with fear, searching for the airplane hangar.

"There it is!" Princess pointed.

Queenie pushed the pedal to the floor, the souped-up engine screaming as the car chewed up the ground. The tires screeched when she smashed the break, the expensive maroon sedan sliding to a stop in front of the closed doors of hangar nineteen. The sisters tore out of the car, knowing every second that passed created more uncertainty about the whereabouts of Pop Somethin'. When they pulled open the hangar doors, they found it empty of an airplane, but what they did find scared the shit out of them.

Pop Somethin' lay on the ground in a pool of blood.

Queenie ran to him, tears streaming down her face as she knelt down next to him. "Pop, get up! Getcho ass up!"

When the big goon didn't move, Queenie began running her hands over his body to check for wounds while Princess put her head to his chest and listened for a heartbeat. "His heart beating," Princess said, breathing a sigh of relief. "He smell like liquor. I think he asleep."

Thankfulness passed through Queenie's body, but just to make sure, she put her head to his chest and listened to his rhythm of life. Jubilation spread across her face. A couple of slaps to the face made him open his eyes.

"Damn, baby. Why you hittin' me like that for?" Pop slurred.

J-Blunt

"Don't be scarin' me like that, nigga. We thought cho ass was dead."

Pop grinned. "Can't nobody kill me. I'm immortal."

"Well, getcho immortal, drunk ass up and let's get the fuck outta here before people start askin' questions 'bout this blood. Whose blood is it?"

"Niggas got convicted and judged," Pop grinned.

After the sisters helped him to the car and lay him in the back seat, the Maserati sped toward the highway. "What we doin', Pop? Where are goin'?" Queenie asked as she maneuvered the sports car.

"And where is C-Note?" Princess asked.

"Nigga got judged for breakin' the G-Code," Pop slurred.

"How the fuck you get to the airport?" Queenie asked.

"I had a meetin' wit' the boss. Texas burnt up. We gotta go."

Princess's head snapped around. "What? Leave Texas? And go where? Why?"

"He gave me 72 hours to go or they comin' at me."

"Fuck Gonzo!" Princess spat. "He don't own shit. He can't make us leave. Nigga bleed just like us."

"Them grenades almost blowin' yo' ass up wasn't enough, huh?" Pop laughed. "This a cartel, Princess. This ain't no neighborhood gang niggas. They got reach and long money. I got the heart of a lion and don't fear nothin' but God, but I ain't stupid. They got a green light on me in three days. I'm leavin'. It's up to you if you wanna roll wit' me. You too, Queenie."

"I'm wit' chu, baby," Queenie spoke up. "Tell me the next move and we gon' make it together."

When Pop didn't respond, Queenie glanced into the back seat. Pop was out like a light.

"That's why that nigga don't drink. He can't handle that shit," Princess laughed.

"So, what you gon' do? I'm leavin' wit' Pop. You comin'?" Queenie asked.

24

A Gangster's Code 2

"I guess I really don't got no choice. We don't got no-where to live and we broke. Fuckin' wit' Pop been good for us so far. Ain't no sense in trynna do somethin' different. Plus, we never left Texas except when we went to Mexico wit' Gonzo. A new state might be good for us. But for now let's get to a hotel and get this nigga cleaned up and sober."

When they found a cheap room for the night, the sisters took Pop inside and cleaned him up. After putting him in bed, Princess left to go buy clothes and hygiene products while Queenie cleaned the blood in the bathroom. She had just finished the walls when she heard Pop talking. When she looked into the room, Pop was lying on his stomach, humping the mattress. A wicked smiled spread across her face as she walked over, ready to bring his dream to life.

"Yeah, Shanice. Mm, baby," Pop moaned.

Shock and awe spread across Queenie's face when she realized Pop was dreaming about fucking his cousin. She stood there, watching him hump away at the mattress, questions flooding her mind. Is that why he was so overprotective of her? Did jealously make him beat up C-Note? Was Shanice the reason he didn't believe in love? Because he was already in love with someone else? Queenie knew liquor released inhibitions and made people tell the truth. Pop was in love with Shanice. Queenie knew it in her gut. The realization made her feel some type of way. She forgot about cleaning the bathroom and sat on the bed, watching Pop sleep.

Princess walked into the room half an hour later, immediately noticing Queenie watching Pop sleep. "That is so fuckin' creepy."

"He in love wit' Shanice."

Princess eyed her sister. "What the fuck you just say?"

"He in love wit' Shanice. That's why he overprotective of her. That's why he beat up C-Note. He was just havin' a dream about fuckin' her. I watched him."

Princess didn't understand the hurt and confusion swirling in her sister's eyes. "How do you know he love her? And why you so upset? It was only a dream."

"He said her name. And I feel some type of way 'cause my nigga in love wit' somebody that ain't me."

Princess sat near her sister. "Don't do this to yo'self, Queenie. This could be in yo' head. Plus, he not only yo' nigga. He mine, too. He fuck me just as much as he fuck you. So what if he fuck somebody else? We got his loyalty."

"It's not in my head. I know what I seen."

"C'mon, sis. Chill. It's me. Don't let this dream get to you. You know how Pop feel about love. It's not in him. Besides, look at us. We been fuckin' since we was twelve. So what if he have a dream about Shanice? At least he didn't fuck her. I don't think."

Queenie side-eyed her sister as she got up from the bed. "You know just what to say to make me feel like shit, bitch."

***

The queasiness of Pop's stomach awoke him from his slumber. When he opened his eyes, he immediately noticed several things. It was dark. He wasn't sure where he was. His head pounded like the Energizer Bunny was beating it instead of a drum. He had to use the bathroom.

After taking a few moments to gather his strength, Pop lifted his head to look around. Queenie was sleeping on the left, Princess on the right. The bathroom was a couple feet from the bed. He made a move to sit up and immediately felt the bile rising. Using a hand to cover his mouth, he leapt from the bed, spilling vomit all the way to the bathroom. He knelt over the toilet, hugging the porcelain and heaving his guts out.

"Damn, Pop! You threw up on me!" Princess whined, heading for the sink.

A Gangster's Code 2

Pop responded with heaves as the contents of his stomach spilled into the toilet. When Princess finished wiping her arm, she put a cool towel on the back of Pop's neck and held his dreads as he finished throwing up. When he was done, he lay on the floor exhausted, loving the way the cold tile felt against his naked skin.

"How much did you drink?" Princess asked, doing a bad job at hiding her giggles.

"I don't know. Gonzo kept pourin' shots. Liquor like a truth serum. I guess he got me drunk to question me."

The mention of liquor making a person tell the truth made Princess think of her sister's story about Pop fuckin' the mattress. "Do we really gotta leave Texas? Where we gon' go?"

"Yeah. I don't know where to go. All I know is Houston. But I can't go to war wit' a cartel wit' me, you, and Queenie."

"Damn, Pop. This is so fucked up. But okay. You my nigga. I'm wit' chu. Tell me what you think. What's our next move?"

Pop was quiet for a few thoughtful moments. "I need to go back to Houston. I gotta holla at Deso."

Princess looked like Pop had just told her to eat a shit sandwich. "Is you crazy? Deso? What about Pop Squad? You know they want cho ass dead, right?"

"Fuck Drama and Snot. I ain't worried 'bout dem niggas, but I need some paper. And a couple swords. Gonzo took my D.E.S. Plus Deso can put us on a move that will pay for us to get where we goin'. This the only thing I can think of on short notice."

Princess leaned against the sink and thought about what Pop said. It wasn't a good plan. In fact, it was terrible and might get them killed, but she didn't have a better one. "Damn, Pop. You bad for a bitch's nerves, nigga. Damn."

"A life without excitement isn't worth livin'," Pop grinned.

"Lately our lives been havin' too much excitement. You ever thought about gettin' a job and makin' us some honest women?"

Pop cut his eyes at her.

Princess burst out laughing. "I'm just fuckin' wit' chu, nigga. Damn. I wish you coulda seen the look on yo' face."

"You got jokes, huh? I told you niggas get killed for playin' too much."

"The way yo' ass laid out on the floor, I ain't worried 'bout you doin' shit. You so weak right now you prolly can't wipe yo' ass."

"Don't let this shit fool you. When a wolf cry, you can still see that wolf teeth."

Princess sat on the edge of the tub, spreading her naked thighs and revealing her pink pussy. "I'm a lioness, nigga. Wolves ain't shit to me."

Pop watched her fingers spread her pussy lips and rub her clit. "So, you sayin' I ain't shit?" he asked, struggling to get to his feet.

Princess shoved a finger in her hole and moaned. "Mm. Yeah, nigga. I said you ain't shit. Fuck you gon' do?"

Pop couldn't make it to his feet, so he crawled over. Princess pulled a finger from her juice box and forced it into his mouth. "Yeah, nigga. That's right. Stay on yo' knees and worship the pussy!"

"Nah, bitch," Pop said, reaching up and wrapping a big hand around her throat. "Get on yo' knees and worship my dick."

While Pop choked her, he used her body and the tub to climb to his feet, but Princess wasn't going to be obedient this time. Before Pop could stand fully erect, she pushed him. Pop lost his balance, letting go of her throat, trying to break his fall. He hit the wall and slid back to the floor. Princess moved quickly, straddling his lap and grabbing two fistfuls of his dreads as she lowered her face a few inches from his.

"Nah, nigga. I ain't bowin' down to you tonight. I'm runnin' this shit. Worship my pussy, nigga." After an aggressive tongue kiss, Princess straddled his face, forcing her pussy onto his lips.

Feeling weak and a little light-headed, Pop gave in. He flicked his tongue across her clit a few times before sucking it between his lips.

"Oh, shit! Yeah, nigga! Anoint yo' lips wit' my pussy juice," Princess moaned, pulling his dreads roughly.

Pop reached up and stuck two finger from his left hand in her ass and two fingers from his right hand in her pussy. He worked his fingers simultaneously in her two holes while continuing to suck her clit. Princess went wild!

"Oh, Gawd! Oh, shit! Shit! Shit! Shit!'' she screamed, digging her hands into Pop's skull and pulling his dreads harder. Even though it felt like she was tearing dreads from his head, Pop suffered the pain, using his hands and mouth to bring her pleasure.

When Princess's orgasm began building, it felt like nothing she had ever felt before. Her body tingled from scalp to toenail. She could feel every nerve in her body responding to the build up. Her skin was burning hot, and it felt like tiny electric insects crawled up and down her body. Then the floodgates released, Princess's body locked, her eyes popped, and jaw dropped. The cum gushed from her body like a rushing river, filling Pop's mouth and washing down his body. "Ooh shit!" Princess screamed, unable to keep her balance and falling clumsily on top of Pop. Even though he was no longer touching her body, Princess continued cumming, her body trembling like she was freezing.

Pop spat out the cum and watched the reaction the orgasm was having on her. He had never seen anything like it. She lay on top of him moaning and cumming for two minutes. When she finished, she lay on top of Pop, drained of energy, unable to move.

"Talk that shit now, lioness. Lemme hear you roar," Pop laughed.

"Fuck you, nigga," Princess breathed.

"That's exactly what I plan on doin'."

Pop pushed Princess's limp body onto the floor and climbed between her legs. She was so wet he slipped easily into her pussy. The penetration into her already sensitive pussy made her cum again.

"Oh, shit, Pop! Oh, shit!" she sang.

He could feel her body locking up, pussy contracting and getting wetter. The feel of her insides and the sound of her moans seemed to make Pop stronger. He could feel the weakness leaving and strength returning to his body. The short, shallow thrusts turned into deep, long strokes. It wasn't long before both legs were on his shoulders and he was drilling her pussy like a mad man. Princess came so many times she lost count. To her it seemed like every time he pushed inside, she came.

When Pop felt strong enough, he got up and spun Princess around, leaning her over the tub. Princess's body went numb as Pop fucked her from behind. When he felt himself about to bust, he pulled out of her and moved Princess to sit on the toilet. His dick was slick with pussy juice as he pushed it in her face. Princess sucked him slowly, unable to give much effort.

"That's right, Princess. Worship yo' king's dick. Bless yo' tongue wit' my holy seed," Pop encouraged, using a hand to guide her head. When her effort didn't match what Pop wanted, he grabbed two handfuls of her dreadlocks and began fucking her face. Princess gagged and slobbered as Pop stuffed his dick in and out of her throat. When he felt himself about to bust, he pulled out of her mouth and began jacking off. Thick, white sperm erupted from his body, splashing onto her forehead. Pop used his tool to rub it in.

"Yeah, baby. Lemme anoint you wit' my holy water."

Movement near the door made Pop look over. Queenie stood there, watching the action. "That shit was sexy as fuck. I hope that wasn't all you got, 'cause I want mines, too."

J-Blunt

Chapter 3

In the summertime, Houston's Fifth Ward was alive like a sell-out event had come to town. Nonstop activity of every kind flooded the neighborhoods. They sold weed at this house, dope in the house across the street, and heroin up the block while women of all ages and body types used what God gave them to catch a check. In the midst of it all, children navigated the blocks, avoiding hot spots and compromising situations like they were dodging land mines, not allowing the criminal activity that was a normal part of their lives to dim their desires to have fun and be kids.

With all the action happening around them, nobody paid much attention to the maroon Maserati as it pulled to a stop in front of a brown and yellow house in the middle of the block. Princess and Queenie climbed from the passenger and rear seats dressed in identical body-hugging white cat-suits and red bottoms, their dreads hanging loosely down their backs. The white fabric on their curvy black bodies made them look like sinful angels. Everyone within a hundred feet stopped what they were doing to get an eyeful of the dark-skinned beauties.

When the driver's door opened, Pop Somethin' stepped out of the car, a snug-fitting white t-shirt showed his muscular physique, fitting white jeans and white Jordans completing the Ice Cream Man ensemble. If the sight of the women made everyone want to get close, the sight of the goon made them recoil in fear. Everyone in the Fifth Ward knew who Pop Somethin' was, even if it was their first time seeing him. His lore was passed down through stories to all like Jesus dying on the cross to save sinners from hell was taught in every Christian church in America.

"Damn, Pop. Why they lookin' at us like that?" Queenie asked, noticing the way they were being watched.

"Back when Egypt ruled the world, when the kings returned from battle, the people flocked to the streets, celebrating and paying homage. They all know the king has returned."

Princess rolled her eyes and mumbled something under her breath.

"You got somethin' to say, Princess?" Pop asked.

She cleared her throat and tried to speak, voice sounding like a hoarse whisper. "Get off that damn high horse, nigga."

"I can't hear what you sayin'. Worshippin' yo' king and prayin' to my dick must've put a strain on yo' voice, huh?" Pop laughed.

"Can we just go in the house before somebody that know Pop Squad call them niggas?" Queenie said.

After walking up on the porch and knocking on the door, a woman's voice called from inside, "Who is it?"

"Pop Somethin'. Open the door."

Four locks clicked and the door swung open. A short, curvy, light-skinned woman with graying hair stood in the doorway. At first glance she seemed like a respected, mature woman who, back in her day, had many male admirers, but looking into her eyes revealed something more. Like a Transformer, there was more to this woman than met the eye. She looked Pop Somethin' over from head to toe, mean-mugging him. Then she opened her mouth to speak, revealing open-faced gold teeth on her top and bottom rows. "Nigga, you been out all this time and this yo' first time comin' to see me? If you wasn't so big and I wasn't old, I'd jump up and bust you in yo' shit. Now bend down and gimme a hug."

Pop bent down and swallowed the older woman in his arms. "'Sup, Aunty Dorothy? See you still talkin' like you can whoop me," Pop laughed.

"That's 'cause I can. You might have er'body scared of yo' big ass, but I ain't. And damn, you done got bigger. Shanice said you got bigger, but I didn't know you got this damn big," she said, stepping back to look at him again.

A Gangster's Code 2

"Milk do a body good."

"Speakin' of milk, who y'all s'posed to be? The milk man and his two milk maids?" Dorothy laughed.

"I'm the Ice Cream Man, and these my bitches, Queenie and Princess. Now, you gon' let us in or make us stand on the porch all day?"

Aunty Dorothy cut her eyes at him. "Boy, don't be talkin' to me like that! I just tol' yo' big ass I ain't scared o' you. Now, c'mon in," she said, stepping aside to let them pass. Then she stepped onto the porch to address the onlookers. "Yeah, muthafuckas! My nephew back now. Talk that shit if you want to and see, won't they be puttin' y'all in Ziploc bags.

"Yo' aunty crazy," Queenie laughed.

"You ain't seen shit yet."

After locking the door, Aunty Dorothy turned to her guests. "Y'all sit down. Y'all want somethin' to drink? I got some Crown Royal."

"We will take a drink," Queenie and Princess spoke.

"You know I don't drink, but I'm hungry. What you got in there to eat?" Pop asked.

"Some corn beef I made last night. Want me to make you a sammich?"

"*A* sammich?" Pop asked, wondering why she only mentioned making one.

"Boy, you ain't finna eat up all my damn food. I got a man that gotta eat, too. Megan and my granddaughter s'posed to come over later, and I gotta feed my baby."

Pop pulled a half ounce of lime-green weed from his pocket, shaking it in his aunty's face.

Everything she said went out the window when she seen green. "Shit, why you ain't pull that out when you walked in? You can have as many sammiches as you want if you gimme half of that sack."

After fixing Queenie and Princess drinks and making Pop Somethin' four corned beef sandwiches, they all sat around and got high.

"Now, you know I love you, nephew, and you can come by my house anytime you want, but tell me why you really here. Shanice called me the other day talkin' 'bout you and that boy she fuckin', C-Somethin', was in trouble. How bad is it?"

"I took care of er'thang, but I gotta leave Texas in a couple days. I just need somewhere to lay my head at 'til I catch up wit' a few niggas. I need some heat. You got somethin' I can hold until I get right?"

Dorothy smiled. "You just in time. My man bought me a Mac-11 that I don't want. I don't need no damn machine gun. My 380 just right for me."

"You a lifesaver, aunty."

A knock on the door interrupted their conversation. At the same time, Aunty Dorothy's phone rang.

"Where that Mac at? I'ma get the door," Pop said.

"In the kitchen. Top shelf, above the refrigerator. This Shanice on the phone. Wanna talk to her?"

Pop didn't respond to his aunty's question as he went to get the Mac. The black semi-automatic was fully-loaded with a 32-shot clip. He pushed off the safety as he walked to the front door. "Who is it?"

"2-Tone."

Pop looked out the peephole and seen a light-skinned nigga with brushed waves standing on the porch. After tucking the Mac under his shirt, he opened the door. Before he could speak to the stranger, Aunty Dorothy got his attention.

"Yo' cousin want to talk to you, Paul!"

"Not right now," he said before addressing 2-Tone. "What' up, boy? See you still out here."

"I thought that was you, nigga. Damn! You big as a muthafucka!" he said, looking Pop from head to toe like he was a god. "Fuck you get out, nigga?"

"Shit, a minute ago. I was fuckin' around in Dallas. Just came through on my way outta town."

"Fo' sho. Fo' sho. You still into that same shit you was on before you got locked up? I know some niggas that–"

"Paul, Shanice wanna talk to you," Aunty Dorothy interrupted, walking over and holding out the phone.

"Not right now. Tell her I'ma call her back."

"Nah, Pop. Talk to me now," Shanice said through the speaker phone. "Where C-Note? Why he not answerin' the phone?"

"I don't know," Pop mumbled.

"What you mean, you don't know? He was s'posed to come get you and y'all was s'posed to come get me. That was two days ago. What happened?"

"I told you, I don't know. I'ma call you later," Pop said before walking off the porch.

"You good?" 2-Tone asked, noticing the change in Pop's demeanor.

"Yeah. I'm good. Tell me what chu talkin' 'bout? You got a move you trynna put me up on?"

"Not me. Some niggas in the Third. Born Ready. The shit he on a li'l too much for me, but I can put him on yo' line."

"Do that. Take down my number and get at me."

***

"I don't mean to get in yo' family business, Pop, but don't you think you should at least talk to Shanice and put her mind at ease?" Queenie asked from the passenger seat.

"If you don't mean to get in my family business, why you gettin in it?" Pop mugged.

Queenie rolled her eyes and sucked her teeth. "Because I would want to know if I was her. She pregnant, and the stress might hurt the baby. Just tell her he dead so she can start to heal."

"You want me to tell her I killed the nigga, too? That I cut his head off and gave it to Gonzo?"

Queenie rolled her eyes, turning to look out the window.

"She do got a point," Princess spoke up from the back seat.

"Here we go," Pop breathed. "Fuck y'all s'posed to be on, some keepin'-it-righteous shit? Queenie, is you gon' tell her you fucked her nigga before you blew his brains out? Shanice don't need to know shit. I did her a favor. Niggas ain't shit. Maybe now she get a square-ass nigga like I been told her."

Princess continued speaking her mind. "You can't control her life, Pop. Why you so overprotective of her, anyway? She ain't cho bitch. We is. She a grown woman. Let her live her life."

Pop didn't respond right away. He mugged Princess through the rearview mirror. "I know y'all think what y'all doin' is helpin', but it ain't. I'ma deal wit' this how I see fit, and right now I don't want to talk to her about it. This family bidness, and it don't got shit to do wit' y'all. I got it."

Princess blew him off. "Okay. She gon' hate yo' ass, not me."

Instead of responding to Princess, Pop turned up the radio and let Derez Deshaun's *Hardaway* fill the car. Twenty minutes later he parked the sports car behind a white Range Rover. Outside, the block was filled with kids running around and playing while parents sat on the porch and watched them. Pop, Queenie, and Princess stepped from the car and walked up to a white house with a fenced-in backyard. The wooden gate was seven feet tall, so even Pop couldn't look over it to see what was going on, but the sound of Al Green's *Love and Happiness* and raised voices let him know a grown folks party was in full swing.

"Aye! Come open the gate," Pop yelled, banging on the gate a few times.

"Who out there?" a woman called.

A Gangster's Code 2

"Pop Somethin'. Deso here?"

When the gate opened, a short, dark-skinned woman with a graying afro greeted them. She had bubble eyes and two moles on her right cheek, below her eye. She smiled as she looked the big man from head to toe. "What I tell you 'bout usin' those street names by my house, Paul? God didn't give y'all them names."

He let out a chuckle. "My bad, Aunty Ruby. How you doin'? Is Desmond here? He told me to meet over here."

"I'm doin' fine. Y'all c'mon in. We havin' a get-together. Desmond in the basement with the boys. All the women out here, so you ladies can pull up some chairs to the tables."

The backyard party was in full swing. Women of all ages sat around talking and playing card games and dominoes. When the twins walked in the backyard, a woman screamed and ran over, hugging them like they were long-lost sisters. Pop eyed the woman as she hugged his women. Hair long, dark, and curly, light brown complexion, small waist, wide hips, a big booty, hazel green eyes, thin lips. nice teeth. If he had guessed her race, he would've said Latina. She flexed her banging body off in a white-striped halter top, black leggings, and heels.

"Pop, this our girl, La'Qua," Queenie introduced.

Pop nodded. "'Sup?"

"You, nigga," La'Qua said, looking Pop up and down. "You owe me a couch. Ya blood didn't come out the pillows."

"My bad for that. I was fresh out and not thinkin'. But I'ma take care of that before we leave town."

La'Qua laughed. "I'm fuckin' wit' you, nigga. You good. Deso in the house."

After giving a nod to Queenie and Princess, Pop went in the house and found Deso in the basement. About ten men and boys were lounged around on furniture, all of their eyes on the video game being played on the big screen TV.

"What up, nigga?" Pop called.

Everyone in the basement spun around at the sound of the new voice. When Deso seen Pop, he got up wearing a big smile. "What up, nigga? I see you on yo' snowman shit," Deso laughed, showing the chip on his front tooth.

"Ice Cream Man, nigga. I'm on my Master P shit. No Limit!" Pop laughed as the men embraced.

"C'mon, nigga. Let's go up to the kitchen and kick it," Deso said, leading the way upstairs where they had seats at the kitchen table. "What the fuck you doin' back in Houston, nigga? I thought y'all was fuckin' up Dallas."

"We was. My nigga, that shit was sweet as fuck. I was in wit' a Mexican Cartel, checkin' a bag, rubbin' shoulders wit' the boss. I had damn near half a ticket."

Deso's eyes popped. "Fuck you doin' back in H-Town, nigga? And put me on!"

Pop shook his head. "It fell apart. The nigga that put me in turned bitch. Tried to bring the cartel down on some snitch shit, so I had to judge 'im. The cartel came at me and burned down my house . I lost er'thang. I was gon' check a mil and go back home."

Deso was in awe. "Damn, Pop. You touched a half a ticket, nigga? You was gettin' it, boi!"

"Yeah. Now I gotta get outta Texas. The cartel boss gave me 72 hours yesterday. In two days, they got a green light on me."

"Damn! Nigga, you beefin' wit' a cartel? Shit, Pop. I love you like a brotha, nigga, but I ain't goin' against no cartel. That's suicide."

"Nigga, I ain't stupid. I seen what them Mexicans can do. They got me. Gonzo gave me a pass. I'm leavin' Texas. I came to you for a front. I need a coupla dollas and some heat. All I got is a Mac from Aunty Dorothy."

40

A Gangster's Code 2

"Okay. I got a couple throw-aways, and I can get you a few bands. I'm between moves right now, so shit tight. The squad burnin' up H-Town, so niggas be on point when we come around. I'm thinkin' 'bout movin', too. Niggas been at our heads lately. I think it's a price on our heads, too, 'cause niggas shredded up our whips. Now we stay in rentals. If it ain't tinted, I ain't ridin' in it."

"Yeah, it might be time for you to go, brah. I need anotha shooter since I'm goin' to a new town."

Deso laughed. "The offer is tempting, Pop, but I can't leave my li'l niggas. Drama and Snot would starve wit'out me. Or get killed."

"They big boys. Sink or swim."

"Them my li'l brothas, Pop. I can't do 'em like that. I'ma figure somethin' out."

"Is them niggas still gunnin' for me? Princess said they want my head."

Deso let out a long breath. "Yeah. They young and don't believe in foldin' they hands. You bagged they brotha in front of they face. I can't get 'em to let that go. They don't see he was in the wrong."

"You know you gon' have to bury them niggas if they come at me, right? Queenie and Princess ain't the same bitches they was when they was wit' y'all. They killas now. I think Queenie a homicidal maniac. Killin' make her pussy wet."

Deso burst out laughing. "You bullshittin'! Queenie 'bout that action? She talk shit, but won't bust a trap. A nigga got the ups on us and she hit him in the stomach, but couldn't do him in."

"That shit over, brah. She hit niggas. Princess, too."

Deso laughed again. "Damn. That sound crazy. Fuck you do to my bitches?"

"My bitches," Pop corrected.

"Yeah, yo' bitches," Deso laughed, checking the text he had just received on his phone. "Drama and Snot on they way over. I'ma tell them niggas to fall back so you can get a head start on them niggas."

Pop stood up and looked out the window at Princess and Queenie. They smiled and laughed as they talked to La'Qua. "Nah, let them niggas come through. I'ma offer 'em passes."

"Y'all niggas ain't finna shoot up my aunty house."

"I left the Mac in the car. The clip too long and I know Ruby woulda got at me for bringin' pistols in here. Let them niggas come over. Just make sure they leave they heat in the car."

Deso gave Pop a long look. "A'ight, nigga. Y'all betta not be on no bullshit."

When Deso began typing the text, Pop's phone rang. It was 2-Tone. "What up, brah?"

"I got at Born Ready and told him 'bout you. He already know who you is and wanna meet. I'm headin' that way later. Want me to pick you up by yo' people's house?"

"I'm tyin' up somethin' right now. Gimme a li'l time. I'ma hit you when I get by my aunty house."

"Who was that?" Deso asked after Pop hung up.

"2-Tone. Remember him?"

"Yeah. His soft ass. He still robbin' old bitches for they purses?"

"I don't know. He want me to meet this nigga, Born Ready. Say he got a move. If possible, I wanna get y'all wit' me. That's why I wanna holla at cho li'l niggas."

"I neva heard of that nigga, but I do need a good lie. These niggas should be pullin' up in a minute. Hopefully these li'l niggas can let that shit go."

Movement from Princess and Queenie caught Pop's eye. They went from laughing and talking to wearing mean mugs. When Drama and Snot walked in the backyard, the sisters went to confront them.

"Yo' boys here!" Pop called.

A Gangster's Code 2

Deso went outside and stepped between his boys and the twins, defusing the hostility. Pop leaned against the sink as the men walked in the house.

"Them hos bogus for leavin' the team to fuck wit' dat nigga," Drama spat.

"I should go grab my shit from the car and put it on them hos. They betrayed us," Snot added.

"Sometimes the grass is greener on the other side," Pop spoke up.

The young goons looked at Pop Somethin', then Deso, and back at Pop Somethin'. Surprise showed on their faces before changing to anger. Drama spoke first. "Nigga, you lucky I left my shit in the car or I'd push yo' shit in!"

"They didn't stop makin' guns after they made y'all shit. I'm trynna give you niggas a chance to do somethin' betta than y'all been doin'. I'm offerin' a pass. Keep talkin' shit and I'ma take it back."

Snot made a move like he was about to attack Pop. Deso grabbed his arm. "Chill, brah. Not in my aunty house. Listen to what he gotta say."

"Dat nigga killed Yea! Fuck what dat nigga talkin' 'bout!" Snot yelled, his eyes red with anger.

"You gon' have to get over that, baby boy. That's how it is out here. Niggas play for keeps. But I'm trynna put y'all in a position to win. Fuck wit' me."

"Nah, nigga, fuck you!" Snot mugged. "We play for keeps, too, nigga."

"Yo' mug cute, nigga. Last chance. Let that shit go. Fall back," Pop warned.

"Fuck you, nigga. You dead," Drama mugged.

Snot was done talking. He ran at Pop, his arm cocked back to swing a wild haymaker. When Drama seen his day-one move, so did he. Since Pop's knee was swollen and stiff from the leg kicks, he wasn't as agile as normal. When Snot swung the wild punch, Pop knew he couldn't dodge it, so he took a step forward, taking the punch on his neck and ear. He retaliated with a punch to Snot's solar plexus, taking his breath. He went down instantly, clutching his stomach. Instead of taking advantage of Pop being distracted and throwing punches, Drama grabbed Pop, trying to slam him. Six inches and a hundred pounds difference made it look like Drama was trying to wrestle a bear. Pop easily lifted him in the air and threw him out the window.

"Damn, nigga! What the fuck? I told you niggas to chill!" Deso snapped

"Yo' boys started that shit. You seen I tried to give them niggas passes," Pop defended.

The back door being snatched open got Pop and Deso's attention. Ruby ran into the kitchen, her eyes wide like a mad woman. "Y'all niggas done lost y'all fuckin' minds? Get the fuck outta my house! And somebody betta gimme some money for my muthafuckin' window!"

Chapter 4

"You look like you got a limp," 2-Tone commented as he and Pop walked toward a rundown apartment building in the Third Ward.

"It ain't shit. Knee a li'l sore," Pop said, rubbing his stiff joint.

"Good, because you gon' need them legs. I hear you got a lotta enemies."

Pop gave him a side-eye. "Oh yeah? What you hear?"

"That's the word out here. They say you added a nigga named Yea to yo' body bag count. His cousins be roamin' the Third. It was some shit about a price on yo' head a while back."

"Who is his cousin?"

"Block and Raw. Niggas savages, too."

Pop acknowledged the information with a nod. "Good lookin' on the heads-up. I'ma keep my eyes open. Hopefully they got a nice price on me. I'ma be pissed if it's pennies."

"Last I heard, it was twenty-five bands. Cash money."

Pop laughed. "That ain't shit. My head gotta be worth more than that. I survived a cartel hit."

2-Tone frowned. "Niggas got a price on yo' head and you laughin', brah? Somethin' wrong wit' chu, brah."

When they walked in the building, 2-Tone led the way up to the second floor and knocked on apartment eight.

"Who dat?" a deep voice called.

"2-Tone."

Locks clicked and the door swung open. Before them stood a short, dark-skinned nigga with a bald head and neatly-trimmed goatee. His physique made him look like he could've been a running-back. His eyes were hard and piercing, like he had seen and done a lot. He acknowledged 2-Tone before looking up to Pop. Neither man blinked during the short staring contest. In the millisecond it took them to assess one another, Pop knew Born Ready was cut from a rare cloth. The man's eyes told of wars and battles. Wins and losses. Wisdom gained from the lessons life had tossed at him.

"What up, Born Ready?" 2-Tone smiled.

"What's good, brah?" he said before turning back to Pop. "So, you the nigga that got his name in er'body mouf."

"Only reason my name in they mouth 'cause they ain't got shit to talk about."

Born Ready acknowledged the wise response with a smirk. "Y'all come in. Have a seat. Want somethin' to drink or smoke?"

"I don't drink, but I smoke," Pop said, eyeing the expensive-looking glass chessboard that sat on the table.

"Pour me up and roll me up!" 2-Tone laughed.

"Sasha! We got company. Get us somethin' to drink!" Born Ready called as he sat in the plush, black leather chair.

A few moments later a big-boned woman with jet black skin walked into the living room. She wore a way too small purple silk robe that did a terrible job of hiding her body parts. Her silver hair was cut low with brushed waves, and every time she took a step, all of her jiggly parts jiggled. "Whatcha all want?" she asked, showing a mouth filled with gold teeth.

"Bring us some yak," Born Ready said, firing up a blunt. "I see you lookin' at my board. You play?"

"I'm familiar with the game."

Born Ready laughed. "Helluva response. But did you know that besides being a game of war, chess is also a social game?"

"It's white versus black. I think it shows up in our everyday life all the time, not just on a chessboard."

Born Ready looked impressed. "Novotny interference. This happens when two black pieces obstruct each other's ability to protect vital squares."

A Gangster's Code 2

Pop knew what Born Ready was trying to do. He was feeling out to see the depth of his knowledge, so Pop showed that he read the same book. "Turton doubling. A theme where one black piece falls back, allowing a second black piece to move in front so the two of them can attack the white king together on the same line."

"*The Emperor of Ocean Park.* You read that book, too?"

"I'm familiar with a lot of things."

"What the fuck just happened?" 2-Tone asked.

"Good warriors practice the art of emptiness and fullness. When you make people come to you, their force is always empty. As long as you don't go to them, your force is always full. The Ninth Law of Power."

"That was too deep for him," Pop chuckled. "The first round of a fight ain't about trynna win. It's about gettin' to know who you about to fight."

2-Tone nodded like he understood.

"Okay, Pop. I'ma be real. I ain't met a nigga out here like you. When I was down, you see niggas gettin' sharp, heads in them books. But out here, niggas is on pills and quotin' rap lyrics like they life principles. I see what you is and I wanna fuck wit' chu. I got a three-part plan that I wanna put in motion. None of it easy. And I can't pay up front, but if you fuck wit' me and do me this favor, I'ma do you one in return. Favor for a favor."

Pop laughed.

"What's funny?" Born Ready asked.

"The last nigga that told me that turned out to be a snake."

The men eyed each other, Born Ready judging the depths of Pop's words. "And what happened to the snake?" he asked, passing Pop the blunt.

"Only way to kill a snake is to cut off the head."

Born Ready nodded. "Well, let me rephrase that. I need a nigga wit' cho skills to execute part one of the plan. Part two and three is a group effort. A hostile takeover. After we put our foot down, I'll give you 100 Gs and the option to go yo' way or stay and get rich."

Pop blew out a cloud of smoke, thinking about the offer. "Tell me about part one. Why am I so qualified."

Born Ready smiled. "Because you the only nigga in Texas that I think would succeed breakin' somebody out the joint."

Pop choked on the weed smoke. "Fuck you just say, nigga?"

"My li'l brotha got two hundred years. I want you to break him out."

Pop Somethin' burst out laughing, laughed so hard his stomach began hurting. When he finished, Born Ready spoke up. "I ain't playin', Pop. That's part one."

"How the fuck I'm s'posed to do that? Break in and then break out again? 2-Tone, this what you brought me over here for?"

"Two hundred Gs. Final offer," Born Ready said.

That got Pop's attention. "What you askin' me is impossible."

"Nah, it ain't. He 'bout to have surgery any day. Find out when. Get 'im during transport."

"How the fuck I'm s'pose..." Pop stopped talking when an idea popped into his head. "Tell me his name. Where he locked up at?"

Born Ready smiled again. "They say life is a bitch, right? I think fate the bitch sister. My li'l brotha is Reese Cummings. You know him as Buck Wild."

Born Ready and Pop had another stare down. It was then Pop realized the smaller man was a thinker and force to be reckoned with. And he always appeared to be one step ahead of Pop Somethin'.

"What Buck say about me?"

"Nothin' that ain't true. But Reese lost his appeal. They not gon' eve let my li'l nigga out. I told him when I got out I was comin' to get him. When you stopped talking a second ago, you realized somethin'. What?"

Born Ready was smart and intuitive. Pop knew he would be studied every second he was in the apartment. This was a chess match without using the board. Pop needed to switch angles. "It wasn't shit. How long you been out?"

"A month. But I perfected this plan a long time ago."

"What's part two?"

"I told you. A hostile takeover."

"I gotta leave Texas. Where is this hostile takeover goin' down at?"

"In Atlanta. When I got locked up, my partner took off wit' the loot from our move. I did ten years. Nigga never sent me a penny. Now he up. I'm goin' to collect. Like I said, I perfected my plan. Once you get my brotha, we gone. Me, Buck, 2-Tone, and you."

"Lemme make a few calls and talk to a few people. I'ma get back to you real soon."

"Don't keep me waitin' too long."

"I won't. Time is the currency of life, and I'm still spendin' it."

"Speakin of time, how 'bout we play a game? I ain't had a good challenge since I got out."

Pop Somethin' knew a match with Born Ready would be more than a chess game. It would be a testing of wills. A flexing of their mental prowess and ability to think, strategize, and win. And Pop Somethin' had never met a man he couldn't outwit, outsmart, and outplay. "I got black. Yo' move."

The game of war took longer than anyone expected. Fifteen minutes turned into thirty. Thirty minutes turned into an hour. At some point during the match, both men had almost won and lost. And then, at one hour and seventeen minutes into the game, it was finally decided. Born Ready's face reflected his feelings. His brow furrowed, eyes squinted, lips twisted in a snarl. Pop Somethin's features displayed a similar look.

"Stale mate," Born Ready admitted.

"You can play," Pop Somethin' said. "Next time I won't be so cautious."

"You gotta lose to win!" Born Ready laughed.

***

"Break a nigga outta jail? Nigga, is you crazy? You trynna get us all in the gas chamber?" Princess shrieked.

"We not breakin' him outta jail. It's during transport," Pop explained calmly.

"Oh. Yeah. Well, that makes it a lot better, Pop. Why didn't you say the first time?" Princess said sarcastically. "Talk to yo' man, Queenie. He trippin'."

"I'm wit' my sister, baby. You know you my nigga and I would go to hell and back for you, but this sound crazy. Plus we don't get paid 'til we do the hostile takeover in Atlanta. I don't want a $200,000 I-owe-you. What if somethin' go wrong and we don't get paid? Too many what-ifs."

"I know," Pop agreed, "but what else do we got? Born Ready is a rare kinda nigga. I think this worth takin' a chance on. This might be our chance to get back on our feet."

"You think, Pop. You think. But you not sure. We gotta put too much trust in anotha nigga, and I don't like it," Princess said.

"You know y'all my bitches and I won't tell y'all nothin' wrong. Just like y'all will do whatever necessary to protect me, I will do the same for y'all. My ass is on the line, too. And I got a good feelin' 'bout this. I think this our shot."

"How you gon' find out when the transport is?" Queenie asked.

Pop smiled. "I made a few connections while I was locked up."

A Gangster's Code 2

"I still don't like it," Princess said.

"But what other choice do we got?" Queenie asked, starting to be swayed. "We got 48 hours to leave Texas."

"Listen to what y'all sayin'. This is crazy," Princess continued standing her ground.

"Just gimme some time to see if I can find out the date of transport. If I can do that, then we go from there. Deal? We gon' take it one step at a time."

Princess was about to respond when her phone buzzed. After looking down at the screen, she frowned.

"Who is it?" Queenie asked.

"Uncle Carl. What the fuck he want?" Princess asked before answering. "Hello?" After pausing to listen, she spoke, "Yeah Queenie right next to me." Then a change washed over her face. She went from curious to devastated in the blink of an eye. "What? When? Where is she ?"

"What happened?" Queenie asked, feeling her twin's emotions.

Princess didn't respond. A spaced-out look was in her eyes, and then the tears came.

"What happened?" Queenie yelled, on the verge of crying.

Princess gave her sister the phone. "Momma dead."

Chapter 5

Pop Somethin' wasn't the type to get excited over a female. As far as he was concerned, he was that nigga. A boss. It was a pleasure to be in his presence. But when the hotel door swung open, the boss nigga took a step back and Pop allowed his true desire to take over.

"Damn. You look fresh outta nigga dream."

Nurse Baccara stood in the doorway wearing a black leather corset, black thong, a garter belt, fishnet stockings, and black heels with silver spikes on the toes. Around her neck was a choker with a leash attached. In her hand was a whip. Her dark hair hung loosely in wet curls and she wore light makeup.

"I don't care about your dreams, pig. What do you want? All you blacks are alike. Rapists and murderers. I don't care about your suit and badge. You ain't nothin' without it. Just another piece of shit."

Pop adjusted his aviator glasses, peering down his nose at the Columbian beauty, his other hand resting on the butt of the pistol in his side holster. After a stare down, Pop stepped into the room and grabbed the leash connected to the collar on her neck. After wrapping it around his fist a couple of times, he yanked her into him aggressively and continued pulling until she was standing on her tippy-toes, the choke collar cutting off her air supply. "Who you think you talkin' to like that, bitch? I'll break yo' ass in half! You hear me? You prolly illegal, ain't you? If you don't got a green card, that's yo' ass, bitch."

"Fuck you, asshole," she managed, barely able to breathe or speak. Pop was choking her for real, her face turning red as veins bulged from her neck.

"Get against the wall and let me search you!" Pop demanded, letting go of the leash and pushing her against the wall. After locking the door, he spun around and began an aggressive pat search. He cupped her breasts, rubbed her body, and gripped her bare ass cheeks. Then he moved his hands to the front, digging into her thong and rubbing her pussy.

"Mm!" the nurse moaned. "Stop it, you black bastard! All you want to do is rape me. Stop!"

"Shut the fuck up!" Pop demanded, sticking a finger into her wet pussy.

"No! Stop!"

Pop spun her around quickly, wrapping a hand around her throat. "Didn't I tell you to shut up? Get on yo' knees. I got somethin' to shut you up."

She tried to put up a fight, but Pop forced her to kneel. "No! Fuck you! I won't suck your dick. Fuck you!" she refused, turning her head when Pop stuck his dick in her face.

"You don't wanna suck it? Well, I'ma beat yo' ass wit' it!" Pop said, grabbing his dick like a baseball bat and slapped her in the face. Four dick slaps later, she gave in.

"Okay! Okay!" the nurse cried.

Pop groaned like a bear when she took him in her mouth. The nurse sucked him aggressively, using both hands and lots of slobber. When he had enough, he snatched his dick from her mouth and slapped her with it again.

"You don't deserve to drink my nut. Getcho ass up. Where that muthafuckin' green card? You betta have it or I'm lockin' yo' ass in detention."

"I'm not illegal. I was born here. I'm a citizen."

Pop took a look around the hotel room and seen a suitcase on the bed. There was a combination lock on it. "Open it."

"No."

He snatched the whip from her, holding it over his head. "Open it or I'ma whip yo' ass."

"No," she refused again.

A Gangster's Code 2

Pop grabbed her from the floor and shoved her onto the bed roughly. Then he took the cuffs from his waist, handcuffed her to the headboard, and forced her to kneel face down, ass up. "Tell me the combination."

"No," she said, hiking her fleshy cheeks in the air, anticipating a slap from the whip.

Pop gave her what she wanted.

"Ah!" she screamed as the whip bit into her skin.

"Tell me that combination."

"Fuck you, you black piece of shit. Fuck you!"

Pop whipped her several times, her ass turning pink and red with welts, and the nurse loved it. She kept pushing her ass in the air for more. Pop whipped her harder until she eventually gave in.

"Okay! Okay! I'll tell you. Stop. Please."

When she told him the combination, he opened the suitcase and found it filled with sex toys. Pop rifled through it like he was looking for contraband. "I don't see no ID or Green Card. I'm takin' you to ICE."

"No! No! Please, don't do this. I have to take care of my family. Tell me what you want and I'll do it."

Pop ran the whip lightly up and down her body. The nurse shivered when the leather moved across her stinging ass cheeks. Then Pop grabbed a black mask from the suitcase. It had a large ball where the mouth was that would keep the mask wearer from talking or screaming. "The first thing I want is for you to stop talking," Pop told her as he put the mask on her face.

When he was sure the mask was secure, he flipped her onto her back and ripped off her thong. After forcing her legs open, he grabbed a set of medium-sized anal beads from the suitcase and began kissing his way up her thigh, stopping when her got to her pussy. He kissed the lips a few times before attacking her pearl with his tongue. The nurse went wild as he began inserting the balls into her ass. When he knew she had reached her peak, he began pulling the beads out slowly, continuing to suck her clit. If the ball wasn't in her mouth, the nurse's screams would've made the neighbors call the police.

When her orgasm passed, Pop stood and looked down at her. The nurse was breathing hard, her skin flushed and sweaty. Her eyes were low like she was high and filled with a desire for more sex games.

"I hope you don't think we done," Pop said, licking her cum from his lips.

She couldn't talk because of the ball in her mouth, so she mumbled something, giving him an angry stare. Pop responded by grabbing her arms roughly and unlocking the cuffs. He led her into the bathroom and cuffed her to the shower rod. He left the bathroom for a few moments and came back naked, holding a bottle of sex oil.

"You don't deserve for me to stick my black dick in yo' pussy, so I'ma fuck you in yo' ass until I get fired. And I popped a Viagra, so it might be a while."

***

"Oh my God, that was so hot!" Nurse Baccara moaned, rubbing Pop's chest as they lay in bed.

"I didn't know you had all that freak in you."

"With the right person, anything is possible. I like being around you. When I'm with you, I feel free. You bring out my hidden wants and desires. I would've never done anything like this with Marciano. He would think I'm a nasty slut."

"That's 'cause you fuckin' wit' a chump. Any man that won't let you be you or tries to stop you from experiencing all life has to offer ain't worth yo' time. You a dime, baby. A relationship is about you doin' you, him doin' him, and y'all doin' y'all. If you never feel comfortable enough to express all of you, how can y'all do y'all?"

A Gangster's Code 2

"We can't. And he used to be so cool. But ever since New Orleans he been insecure and acting like a bitch. Always accusing me of cheating and checking up on me. I'm tired of his shit. I want to leave him, but he suicidal. I think he will try to kill us both."

"That ain't no way to live, shawty. For real. How is it you work in a prison and then gotta go home to one? That ain't love. Plus, you been in this hotel wit' me all day. You know that nigga gon' be unhinged the next time he see you. Then what?"

"I don't know. Being with you has been the break I needed. I haven't had good sex since the last time we were together. I can't keep living like this. I need a change. I wish he would just die."

A gleam shown in Pop's eyes. "What if that could be arranged?"

She looked at him questioningly, and then she realized what he was talking about. "No, no, no! I don't mean literally. I don't want him to die. I was just expressing myself."

"What if that is the only way you can be free? What if he keep on stalkin' you and threatenin' you? Like you said, you can't keep livin' like that."

"But death? No, I can't do it."

"Who said you had to do it?"

She studied Pop for a long time. "What are you saying?"

"That I'll do you a favor if you do me one."

"I don't know. I seen shows where people always get caught for this type of stuff. I don't want to go to prison."

"I know what I'm doin', baby. And I'm trynna make yo' life easier. I wanna fuck wit' chu, and I ain't finna be worried 'bout this sucka-ass nigga fuckin' wit' us. If you want what I want, just say the word. You don't need to do nothin' or know nothin'."

"And if I agree to this, what do you want?"

Pop smiled.

***

The gray Durango pulled to the curb of a yellow and white brick house. Marciano stepped out, tired from a long day as a mechanic at an auto parts store. After grabbing the bag of groceries from the back seat, he locked the truck and walked toward the house. He climbed the porch and stuck the key in the lock. As soon as the lock clicked, someone big, fast, and strong moved behind him, locking him in a chokehold. Marciano tried to scream and struggle, but it was no use, the muscular arm wrapped around his throat squeezing like a boa constrictor, taking away his breath and then consciousness.

When Marciano awoke he was in the house, sitting in a chair in his living room. On the table in front of him was a liter of tequila. On the couch across from him was a big man dressed in dark clothing, wearing a ski mask. He also held a big revolver in his fist.

"Who are you?" Marciano asked weakly, rubbing his neck.

"Yo' judge. Drink."

Marciano looked to the bottle of liquor and then back to his 'judge', trying to find something recognizable. A scar. A tattoo. Skin shade. Anything. But the big man was covered in black from head to toe. He even wore gloves on his hands.

"M-my judge? I don't understand."

The big man pointed the gun at him and cocked the hammer. "Shut the fuck up and start drinkin' or I'ma blow yo' shit off."

Marciano reached for the bottle and twisted off the cap. He brought the bottle slowly to his lips and took a sniff.

"That's a new bottle. The faster you drink, the faster we get this over."

"Y-you want me to drink all this?" he stuttered, looking at the bottle like it was poison.

"Either that or I shoot you. Yo' choice."

Marciano took a long drink, the liquor burning as it flowed down his throat. After a pause, he took another and kept at it until half the bottle was gone. "I can't drink any more," he breathed, looking like he was about to be sick.

"Too bad. Drink or you dead."

Marciano began drinking again. He kept taking little sips until most of the bottle was gone, then he lowered it, spilling liquor in his lap as his head lolled around his shoulders like it was about to fall off. Drool spilled from his mouth along with drunken laughter. Pop Somethin' took his cue, getting up and approaching the drunken man. Marciano didn't even put up a fight when Pop put the .357 in his hand. After positioning the pistol to his head, he assisted him in squeezing the trigger.

Pow!

J-Blunt

Chapter 6

"I feel bad about not being there for her," Queenie said, teary-eyed as she watched the casket being lowered into the ground.

"Me too," Princess said, dabbing her eyes with a tissue. "We didn't even know she was sick. She didn't tell nobody. That's what I'm mad about. She didn't even give us a chance to prepare. That was selfish as hell."

The sisters stood beside their mother's grave holding hands, surrounded by family members they hadn't seen or spoken to in years. After a few more words from the preacher, everyone piled in cars and drove to Uncle Larry's house to celebrate Patricia's life. About fifty family and friends gathered inside and outside to eat, drink, and express their condolences. The sisters were sitting on the couch in the living room, nursing drinks while people walked up expressing well wishes and telling stories about their mom.

Neither twin paid attention to the knock on the door. A tall, dark-skinned, balding man walked in and was greeted by the family. When the newcomer spotted the sisters, he made his way over. "Hey, girls," he greeted in a voice barely above a whisper.

Queenie and Princess had their heads down, staring into their drinks, but when they heard the voice, their reactions were instant. Princess's face displayed a rage that would frighten the devil and a host of demons. Her tear-soaked, red-rimmed eyes burned with hate and anger. Queenie's mug was also twisted into a mask of hostility, her breathing harsh, posture tense, and ready to attack.

The newcomer noticed their demeanors and put his hands up, palms out. "I don't mean no harm, y'all. I seen Patricia's funeral on Facebook, and I just wanted to pay my last respects."

Princess's rage was unbridled as she shot to her feet. "Was you thinkin' 'bout that respect when yo' pervert-ass was rapin' us, Chauncey? Fuck you, ho-ass nigga!"

The commotion and loud accusation got everyone's attention. They all looked just in time to see Queenie shoot to her feet and punch Chauncey in the face. Princess's fists flew in rhythm with her sister's as they beat up their childhood monster.

Instead of breaking up the fight, other family members joined in, and they kicked the molester's ass all over the living room. Somehow he managed to get away, but instead of trying to flee through the door, he went right for a window and crashed through it, but getting away wasn't so easy. Some of the hurting family members jumped out the window behind him. Others used the door to run outside, and they all took turns kicking Chauncey's ass down the block. When they got tired of chasing the pedophile, the family members slowly made their way back to Larry's house, gathering on the lawn. After gathering around the twin sisters, Larry got their attention.

"Everybody, listen up. I know we ain't the tightest family, and we done a lot of wrong to each other, but one thang is fo' sho. Don't nobody fuck wit' a Jackson and get away wit' it. Girls, I'm sorry y'all lost y'all momma. That was my sista, and although she had her flaws, she loved y'all. And just know I'ma always be here. We will always be here for y'all 'cause we family. Now, er'body bring it in for a family hug!"

***

Queenie tried to ignore the butterflies fluttering in her stomach as she walked up on the porch of the red and blue house. She had rehearsed the lines several times, hoping to get them right, hoping she would be received with open arms and not hostility. After ringing the doorbell, she fidgeted nervously, waiting.

A Gangster's Code 2

"Who is it?" a woman called from behind the door.

"Queenie."

Two locks clicked and the door swung open. Shanice's eyes were wide with expectation. "Where is Paul?"

"He not here. It's just me."

The expectation in her eyes changed to questions. "Why you here without my cousin? Is it about C-Note? Where is he?"

"I came here to talk. Can I come in?"

"Yeah. C'mon. You want somethin' to drink?"

"Yeah. Sure. Whatever you got."

The women settled at the kitchen table where Shanice poured glasses of sweet iced tea. Queenie noticed that although Shanice tried to look strong, the uncertainty about C-Note was taking a toll on her. Shanice was still and would always be a beautiful woman. The pregnancy had her reddish-yellow skin glowing, hair looking shiny and healthy, and slim and curvy frame looking good in the white yoga pants and t-shirt, but her eyes told a truth her lips didn't have to. The light in them had dimmed, and she had heavy bags underneath.

"Damn, this some good iced tea. Er'thang you do is magic," Queenie said after taking a long drink.

Shanice acted like she didn't hear the compliment. "So, where is my cousin? Do you know where C-Note is?"

Queenie had rehearsed the answer to this question on her way over, and even though she knew what she should say, actually getting the words out was hard. In Shanice's sad eyes she seen hope, and Queenie didn't want to take that away, so she hesitated, unsure what to say.

"Oh, my God! He's really dead? For real?" Shanice asked, the world crashing in her eyes as she collapsed in the chair.

Even though Queenie knew it to be true, she didn't want to be the one to reveal the news. She reached out and took ahold of one of Shanice's hands. "I don't know if he's dead. Pop Somethin' won't talk about it."

"Why not? I thought you was his bitch."

"I am. But he has secrets."

Shanice leveled her eyes at Queenie, staring at her intently. "Tell me the truth. Please. I need to know. What happened to C-Note?"

It took all the willpower Queenie possessed to tell the lie. "I don't know for sure. I thought him and Pop was goin' to take care of the drama, but Pop came back alone. He was bloody and beat up. When I asked what happened, he wouldn't tell me, and he told us not to talk to you. I wanted to reach out to you so many times, but I didn't want to go against my man. He don't even know I'm here now. I just came to let you know I was close by. I'm in Texas for a funeral, and I wanted to let you know I'm here for you if you need anything."

Shanice started to cry. "He's dead. I know it. I can feel it. I just want some closure. This is fucked up. I'ma have two kids without fathers. I hate my life right now."

Queenie went to Shanice and wrapped her in a hug. "Don't say that, gurl. It's gon' get better. I'ma help you any way I can. Just let me know."

Shanice got mad and pushed Queenie away. "How you gon' help me, Queenie? You don't even know me!"

"That don't matter. We sistahs, and sistahs gotta stick together. I got your back. For real."

Shanice's features softened and she began crying again. Queenie closed the distance and wrapped her in a sisterly embrace, rubbing her back and saying soothing words. Then Shanice perked up, her eyes red-rimmed, angry slits. "Paul killed him for snitching, didn't he?"

"What? No, I don't think so. C-Note was his nigga. And he loves you like a sister. He wouldn't do nothin' to hurt you."

A Gangster's Code 2

Shanice lay her head against Queenie and began crying again. "It just don't make no sense."

"I know. But I'll be here for you and those kids. I promise," Queenie said, caressing Shanice's back and neck. When her hand moved to the side of Shanice's face, the caress became tender like that of a lover. To Shanice, Queenie's hands were warm and comforting and slightly erotic. When she felt Queenie's lips on her forehead, surprise flooded her body. Another kiss on her temple made her body stiffen. Another kiss on her cheek. Her ear. Her neck. And then her lips. Queenie's lips were soft as cotton, and the tender kiss sent a shock through Shanice's body.

"What the fuck you doing?" Shanice yelled, shooting to her feet as a new kind of excitement danced inside her.

Queenie lifted her arms, palms out. "I'm sorry. I don't know what. Somethin' just came over me. I got caught up in the moment, I guess."

"I don't do girls, Queenie. I ain't gay."

"I know. I'm sorry. I didn't mean to do that. Are you okay?"

"I'm okay. I'm good," Shanice said, refusing to look Queenie in the eyes as she tried to get her breathing under control.

Queenie noticed Shanice's skin flush and breathing increase. "You sure you okay?"

"Yeah. My hormones are crazy from this baby. Uh, I don't mean to be rude, but I have something to do. Can you tell Paul to call me? I just want to know what he knows. I need closure."

"I will tell him, but don't get your hopes up. Whatever he seen changed him. He not the same. Since he loves you so much, he might be avoiding you 'cause he don't want to 'cause you no pain. But I will try to get him to talk to you. Promise."

"Thanks."

"And make sure you let me know if you need anything. I don't care what it is, how big or how small. Let me know, okay?"

Shanice finally looked Queenie in the face again. The dark-skinned woman's eyes showed temptation, as well as trust and loyalty.

"Okay. I will."

Queenie couldn't wipe the smile from her face as she walked off Shanice's porch. She had accomplished more than she expected. A few more run-ins and Shanice would be hers. Then she could take her to Pop Somethin'. In return, Pop Somethin' would finally give Queenie the love she deserved.

***

"How was the funeral?" Pop asked, kissing Princess as she lay in bed next to him.

"Boring. My momma died."

"At least she didn't feel it. I think heart attacks happen fast."

"We didn't even know she had a heart problem. She was waiting to get open heart surgery. She never even told us she was sick," Queenie said, lying on the other side of Pop.

"She prolly thought she was doin' y'all a favor by not sayin' nothin'. She prolly didn't want y'all to worry."

"We ain't kids no more," Princess said angrily. "She shoulda told us."

"I don't even wanna think about momma no more. How you been, baby? Did you figure out what our next move is?"

"Yeah. Surgery is next week. I want to drive by the hospital tomorrow so y'all can see the layout. I went already. Twice. But y'all need to see for yo'self."

"What about security? They got guns?" Princess asked.

"Yeah. But we got somethin' they don't."

A Gangster's Code 2

The twins looked at him expectantly, waiting to know the secret weapon they possessed.

"The element of surprise. Nobody never tried this before, so they won't be expectin' it. Plus it's two of them and three of us."

"And you think we can get away with it? For sure?"

"One hundred percent. And as soon as we make the move, we on to Atlanta," Pop said confidently.

"Okay, Pop," Princess breathed, "'cause I'm ready to leave Texas. We past them 72 hours, and I don't wanna be worried about no li'l Mexicans trynna blow me up again."

"Amen to that," Queenie agreed.

It didn't take the lovers long to fall asleep. In the middle of the night, Princess was awakened by the need to pee. After relieving her bladder and washing her hands, she went to the kitchen for something to drink. She was about to open the fridge when a shadow at the window got her attention, and then it moved on, followed by two more.

Panic surged through her body as she raced back to the room. She was about to shake Pop awake when another shadow popped up in the bedroom window. She realized they were trying to see in the house, but the closed shades didn't allow it.

When she nudged Pop, he awoke instantly. "What?"

"Somebody outside. It's a lot of 'em. I think it's Gonzo."

Pop slipped into his boxers and grabbed the Mac-11 from under the bed at the same time. "Wake up, Queenie. Strap up and stay out the way. I'ma go check on my aunty," Pop said, keeping the Mac ready as he moved down the hall toward his aunty's room. He opened the door slowly and spotted Dorothy sleeping peacefully. He moved to her bedside to wake her and noticed her window was open. He went over to close the shade and found himself staring into the eyes of a masked stranger.

J-Blunt

Instincts took over and the Mac began spitting. Three shots to the face felled the window peeper.

"Paul! What the fuck?" Dorothy screamed, shooting up in bed with wide eyes.

"Getcho shit! Niggas got the house surrounded!" Pop said, closing the blinds and ducking. As soon as he hit the floor, automatic gunfire sprayed the window, shattering the glass and tearing up the blinds. Pop low-crawled around the bed and dragged his aunty into the hallway, and that's when the front door came crashing in. Pop jumped up and raced to the living room, the Mac-11 spitting fire as fast as his finger could squeeze the trigger. Three people in dark clothes carrying automatic rifles rushed in. A volley of 9mm bullets met them at the threshold, dropping two of them. The last one was able to get off some shots, forcing Pop to fall back in the hallway and duck for cover. The gunman continued to lay down heavy fire as he was followed into the house by two more men. They stopped at the entrance to the hallway, uncertain what to do next. The hallway was empty and there were four closed doors before them.

"C'mon," one of them spoke, taking point. The others followed, keeping their guns ready. They stopped at the first door and leveled their guns. The man on point kicked it open, and instead of waiting to see if anyone was in the room, they began shooting. They sprayed the walls, dresser, and bed with high-powered rifle bullets.

When they were sure the room was empty, they moved on to the next room. After kicking open the door, they filled the room with bullets like they had done the previous one. And while they made noise and wasted bullets, the bathroom door opened. Pop had the Mac-11 and his aunty had her .380. They squeezed the triggers as fast as their fingers could. The ambushers screamed as they were gunned down.

"Who the fuck is they, Paul?" Dorothy whispered.

"I'm 'bout to find out," Pop said, keeping the Mac ready as he crept toward the fallen bodies. Two of them were dead.

68

A Gangster's Code 2

One was alive, but in bad shape. Pop snatched the mask off, surprised at the sight of the light-skinned black man.

"Who the fuck is you, nigga?" Pop asked, pointing the Mac in his face.

"F-fuck you, n-nigga," he mugged.

Pop knew he didn't have much time to get what he wanted, so he grabbed the man by the leg and dragged him into the kitchen. Queenie and Princess were right behind him. Pop gave them orders as he dug in the drawers for silverware. "Turn on all they eyes and put spoons and forks on the fire."

The twins moved fast. It didn't take the metal utensils long to heat up. Queenie put on an oven glove and grabbed a hot spoon. She stuck it on one of the man's eyes and held it in place. The man let out a death scream as his flesh burned.

"Who the fuck sent chu, nigga?" Pop demanded.

The man was in so much pain from the bullets and eye burning he couldn't talk, so Queenie grabbed a red-hot fork and stabbed him in the other eye. The man screamed and his body shook as he grabbed the hot fork from his socket.

"Tell me who sent chu, nigga, and this can be over."

"Okay, mane! Okay! Block said you killed his cousin."

Pop Somethin' connected the dots quickly and then blew the man's mouth apart with ten bullets to the face. Then he went to find his aunty. She was still in the hallway, standing a few feet from the dead bodies.

"What the fuck you done brought to my house, nephew?" she asked, a spaced-out look in her eyes

"I'm sorry 'bout this, aunty. Niggas got a price on my head. I'ma take care of er'thang. Take the Mac. When the police come, tell 'em you did this. They not gon' believe you, but you gotta stick to the story. This yo' house. You got the right to defend yo'self. Princess! Queenie! Let's go!"

J-Blunt

Chapter 7

The white Cadillac truck coasted through Houston's Third Ward, bass-pounding music vibrating the pavement as the sun glistened off thirty-inch chrome wheels. Behind the steering wheel, Block rapped along with Pusha T as he puffed a blunt. The dark-skinned goon didn't look the part of a hustler. He looked more like a shooter: nappy dreadlocks, designer clothes that were wrinkled like he slept in them, and shoes that were expensive, but dirty.

"What it do, fool?" he asked when the passenger door opened.

Raw climbed into the truck looking like he had stepped off a print add in pink and purple Ferragamo from head to toe. "Shit. Still trippin' off the whole team goin' down like that. I heard that nigga was savage, but I didn't know he got down like that. He put all six in a pine box. Fuck this nigga is, Black Panther?"

Blocked mugged his day-one. "This nigga ain't no muthafuckin' superhero, and we gotta get 'im out the way. Them niggas just didn't know what they was doin'."

"You know the sayin', my nigga. If you want somethin' done right, you gotta do it choself," Raw said, pulling out his phone. After dialing a number, he waited.

"What's good?"

"This Raw. What's good?"

"You. I see yo' niggas came and made the block hot as fuck."

"Yeah. You know how we do. But look, I need you to come through for me again. I know Pop Somethin' ain't gon' lay his head back at his aunty house. I got five racks for his new spot."

"C'mon, Raw. You still owe me from tellin' you he was over these ways. You said the price on his head was twenty-five. You gave me ten. When I'ma see that otha fifteen?"

"As soon as we put the nigga in a box, I'ma give you anotha five. That twenty-five was the price on his bead. You gotta pull the trigger to get the prize. Ten was more than enough for that info. Find out where the nigga layin' his head at again and I got anotha five. I drop it off right now."

"I got a betta deal," he countered. "I know where the nigga at right now, but that price went up to fifteen. He layin' low, and if y'all make a move and miss, he gon' know I said somethin' 'cause only a few people know where he at. Gimme fifteen and I'ma bless you."

"C'mon, brah. You my nigga from way back. Don't do me like that. Fuck wit' me."

"Listen, Raw. This bidness, brah. That nigga gon' kill me if he find out I gave you the drop. You see what he did to yo' niggas. Y'all sent a team and they couldn't touch him. I need that fifteen, and time is runnin' out. Next week he pullin' a move and goin' to Atlanta. I'm s'posed to go wit' 'im, but if you hit my hand, fuck Pop and the ATL."

Raw looked over at Block. "He say fifteen. We only got a coupla days before they make a move and hit Atlanta, but he know where he at right now. Fo' sho'."

"Tell him we goin' to get the money now."

"You heard him?" Raw asked into the phone.

"Yeah. But I ain't sayin' shit 'til I got fifteen in my hand. My life on the line, nigga. It's C.O.D. Cash on delivery."

Raw laughed. "A'ight, scary-ass nigga. We got you. Tell me where you at?"

After stopping at a trap house to pick up the money, Block drove toward the meeting spot. He pulled up to a stop light, looking over at the tan Chrysler 300C that pulled alongside the Escalade. A pretty, dark-skinned woman with long dreadlocks winked and smiled up at him from the passenger seat. Then she turned toward the driver, who looked exactly like her, and said a few words. After a laugh, the women smiled and waved at the Cadillac truck.

"Look, brah!" Block said, getting Raw's attention.

Raw looked over just in time to see the identical twins share an aggressive tongue kiss. Block blew the horn and signaled for them to let down the window. Instead of doing so, the sisters waved again. And when the light turned green, the 300C raced off.

"Follow dem hos!" Raw yelled.

Block pressed the gas pedal to the floor. "You think I ain't, nigga?"

After a short chase, they ended up side-by-side at another stoplight. Not wanting to let them get away again, Block parked the truck and got out. He knocked on the window and waited for the smiling dark-skinned beauty to roll it down.

"Hey, baby," Queenie smiled. "You got a fast truck."

"Fuck that. What kinda sistas kiss each other?"

"The freaky kind!" Queenie winked, leaning over and kissing Princess again.

"Get that info, brah!" Raw called from the truck.

Block lifted a hand to Raw, signaling him to relax. "Chill, brah. I got it." Then he turned back to the twins. Queenie was pointing toward the intersection. Block turned and seen the light change to green. The Chrysler's engine revved and tires squealed as the car sped away.

"Ooh, them hos bad!" Block yelled excitedly, climbing back into the truck. A high-speed cat-and-mouse chase played out in the busy streets of Houston. Five minutes later the 300C pulled to a stop in front of an apartment complex. The truck parked close to the bumper. Block and Raw jumped out at the same time as Queenie and Princess.

"Aye, stop playin' wit' me, shawty! Me and my nigga want y'all time. I'm Block. Who is you?" he asked, walking toward Princess.

"How you know we want y'all to have our time?" Princess sassed.

"'Cause we the hottest shit in H-Town! I'm Raw. What up? Who is y'all?"

"I'm Queenie. That's my sister, Princess."

"What kinda twin sistas kiss each other like that?" Block asked.

Princess walked up to him and grabbed his dick through his jeans, teasing him. "Wouldn't you like to know?"

Block grabbed her arm. "Hold on, shawty. Fuck wit' cho boy one time. What up?"

Princess eyed him from head to toe like she was judging his worth. "A'ight, Block. Tell me why me and my sister shouldn't go in the house and fuck each other and leave you niggas out here wonderin' who pussy taste the best?"

"'Cause y'all some boss-ass bitches and we some boss-ass niggas. Show us a good time and we gon' show y'all a good time. One hand washes the other, and both of 'em wash the face."

Princess looked over at her sister. "What you wanna do, Queenie? You wanna get in they truck and fuck these niggas' worlds up?"

Queenie looked Raw over from head to toe, then back at her sister. "Let's fuck 'em up, bitch!"

Inside the Escalade, Queenie got in the back seat with Raw while Princess stayed up front with Block. "So, now that we wit' ch'all, what's the plan?" Princess asked.

"We gotta drop off this paper, and then we goin' to chill in a Presidential Suite. Y'all ever been in one of dem?" Block asked.

"Nah. But that shit sound like we should be there all night! We Presidential bitches!" Princess laughed.

"We gon' grab some Aces and loud and then do it," Raw added, reaching over and gripping Queenie's thigh. She was wearing a tight little black dress with no panties underneath.

74

A Gangster's Code 2

When his hand gripped her thigh, she opened them wide, giving him full access.

"Don't go halfway, nigga. Pet the pussy cat so she can purr for you."

Raw moved a hand further up her thigh and flipped his fingers across her clitoris. Queenie let out a small moan, inviting him to do more. "Damn, Raw. Yo' sexy ass got my pussy wet as fuck. Since y'all truck tinted, stick yo' head down there and let me wash yo' face."

Raw gave his boy a look, asking his approval. When Block nodded, Queenie lay back in the seat and opened her legs wider. Turned on by thoughts of how Queenie would return the favor, Raw dove in headfirst. He wasn't that good at eating pussy, but Queenie moaned like his tongue game was the best she ever had. A couple minutes later Block got their attention.

"Aye, we finna pull up on this nigga right now. Y'all hold on."

When the truck slowed down, Queenie pushed Raw's head aside and grabbed her purse. After stopping at the curb, a light-skinned nigga with brushed waves walked up. Queenie moved to the last row to make room when he climbed in the truck. 2-Tone acknowledged the women with a nod before getting down to business.

"What up? You got my shit?"

Block went in the console and threw him a stack of money. "Yeah, nigga. It's all there. Tell us what we need so we can get on our bidness."

2-Tone fanned through the money. Three stacks, five thousand in each. "Yeah. This what I'm talkin' 'bout! He stayin' wit' this nigga, Born Ready. Y'all gotta be careful 'cause Born Ready ain't to be fucked wit'. Nigga one of them niggas that got a backup plan for a backup plan. A-to-Z-type nigga."

"What the address is? How many people in the house?" Raw asked.

"Born Ready got a bald-headed, black-ass, cornbread-thick bitch, and Pop got two badass twin sis–"

2-Tone stopped talking. His eyes shifted to Princess. She smiled, giving the 'Yeah, it's me' look. Instead of speaking his mind, he turned to look in the rear seat. Queenie pointed a baby 9mm in his face.

"I swear to God, niggas is so stupid!" she laughed.

"What the fuck you doin' wit' that?" Raw asked.

Princess pulled a black 357 revolver from her purse. "Stop playin'. Y'all know what this is. Pussy got you niggas slippin'."

"What the fuck is this?" Block asked.

Queenie looked at 2-Tone. "Tell him."

2-Tone hung his head. "Fuck. These Pop bitches."

A car pulling up behind the truck got Block and Raw's attention. Pop Somethin' climbed out of the 300C looking like a vision in someone's nightmare. Raw knew it was do or die, so he went for the pistol on his waist. Queenie shot him in the face.

Terror washed over Block's face when he seen his boy fall into the seat with a hole in his cheek. Then he looked at Princess.

"Try me and I'ma burn yo' ass, fuck-nigga," she said, cocking the hammer. "Keep yo' hands on the steering wheel."

Pop Somethin' yanked open the side door and took in the scene. Then he began barking orders like a drill sergeant. "Block, come back here and let my bitch drive. Princess, gimme that dog and get us outta here."

When the seating was arranged, Pop was sitting in the rear seat with Queenie. Block, 2-Tone, and Raw's dead body were in the middle row while Princess drove.

Pop addressed 2-Tone first. "I thought we was on the same page, brah? How much he give you for my head?"

A Gangster's Code 2

"C'mon, Pop. It–"

Pop put the revolver to his head. "Think about lyin' to me and I'ma splatter yo' boy shirt."

"F-fifteen racks."

Pop laughed. "That's all I'm worth, Block? Fifteen racks!"

Block wore a salty mug, his hands crossed over his chest. "You know how it is out here, nigga. Quit playin'. You got li'l cuz out the way. Make up yo' mind and do what you got-ta do, 'cause if I make it out this truck, I'm bringin' it to you."

Pow!

A hole the size of a quarter opened up in Block's face, some of his blood spraying 2-Tone. The backstabber let out a scream. "Ah, shit! Damn! C'mon, Pop Somethin'. I didn't mean to do this, mane. I got caught up. Please, don't kill me."

"Shut the fuck up, nigga," Pop spat. "Princess, take us to Born Ready. I need him to see this."

When they got to Born Ready's apartment, Pop sent him a text. The short, bald man came out a few moments later. Pop opened the side door and let him survey the scene. When he seen the dead bodies, his eyes popped and he backed away from the Escalade.

"What the fuck is this, Pop?

"Yo' boy tried to set me up. These dead niggas paid him. They sent them niggas to my aunty house. My bitches caught this nigga gettin' his payment to send these niggas to yo' house next. Matter fact, where that money at, nigga?" Pop said, searching 2-Tone's pockets and taking the fifteen grand.

The concern on Born Ready's face changed to anger in the blink of an eye. "You's a real fuck-nigga, 2-Tone. Foul-ass nigga. Niggas like you don't deserve to breathe."

"C'mon, Born Ready. It ain't like that, brah. I was just trynna-"

"Shut the fuck up, pussy-nigga!" Born Ready exploded. "Lemme see that saw, Pop."

When he gave him the revolver, Born Ready emptied it into 2-Tone's face and chest.

"I'ma take care of all this and get back wit' chu later," Pop said. "Keep yo' enemies close."

"Friends closer," Born Ready finished.

A Gangster's Code 2

Chapter 8

Jason Aldean's country song *Dirt Road Anthem* played softly from the speakers of the state-issued white prison transport minivan. In the driver's seat was Correctional Officer Frank Davis, a 25-year vet of the Texas Department of Corrections. The 56-year-old pink-skinned, silver-haired, man could've retired five years ago, but he wanted to fill his retirement fund to the max, so he planned to stay on the job until he was 65. All he had to do was drive inmates to court, medical appointments, and different institutions.

Arlo Martinez sat in the passenger seat bopping his head to the up-beat country song. Officer Martinez wasn't a fan of country music, but he liked the modern sound and tapped his hand on his knee in rhythm to the music. For the younger prison guard, working transport was a blessing. He didn't have to watch inmates, do cell searches, break up fights, or enforce petty-ass prison rules. Today he could take a break, watch cable, and flirt with the nurses.

"Turn that bitch-ass shit off," an inmate complained from the back seat.

"C'mon, Cummings. It ain't that bad," Officer Davis laughed. "It sounds like that hippy-hoppy stuff, don't it?"

"Hell nah. This hillbilly-ass shit hurtin' my ears. Change the station, Martinez. Fuck that honky."

The 36-year-old Mexican guard began laughing, not wanting to get involved in the radio beef. Davis was a senior officer, and Reese Cummings was no average inmate. He was serving a 200-year sentence for a home invasion and police shooting, and if the violent crime wasn't scary enough, his physical presence was: 6'4" and 250 pounds. Back at the prison he was called Buck Wild, one of the founding members of the violent prison gang ABK, which meant 'Anybody Killas'. The big man's complexion was light brown like sand on a beach, his face and head clean-shaven, and tattoos covered his neck, chest, and arms. Across his face were tales of many prison battles he'd survived, leaving healed scars above his left eye, another above his top lip, and his nose crooked from being broken twice.

"Hey, cool it wit' the insults, boy!" Davis yelled, turning red with anger. "I voted for Obama. Twice. I'm on y'all's side."

"I ain't trynna hear dat shit. Change the muthafuckin' station. And if you call me anotha 'boy', I'ma slip these cuffs and break yo' old ass in half."

"See, I tried to be nice. Since you wanna fuck with me, I'ma fuck with you, stupid nigger," Davis laughed, turning the radio up louder and singing along to the music.

It was 5:47 AM when the prison transport van pulled into the hospital parking lot. Davis drove past the Emergency Room doors and into the underground parking. Prisoners were taken into the hospital through a secure door, out of sight from the civilians.

"Alright, we're here. I don't want no shit out of you, Cummings," Davis said as he parked near the secure entrance.

Buck Wild laughed, flexing his muscles. "Don't get scared now, cracka-ass cracka."

Davis spun around quickly, his face red with anger. "I'll turn this fuckin' van around right now and take your ass back! I don't want anymore shit from–"

The van's passenger window exploded, and officer Martinez was ripped through it. Everything happened so fast the older prison guard didn't realize what was happening. A second later the gravity of the situation dawned on him. The transport van was under attack! He went for the gun at his belt as he spun around, and that's when he noticed the figure dressed in black standing in front of the van, pointing an assault rifle at him. For a moment Officer Davis thought about

80

A Gangster's Code 2

being a hero, then his wife, children, and grandchildren's faces flashed in his mind.

"Put cho hands up!" the rifle-holder ordered.

Davis did as he was told. When the side door opened, a large man dressed in black threw Martinez's unconscious body into the van like he weighed fifty pounds. After disarming the old man, the big man grabbed the old-timer and threw him in the back seat with Martinez. Then the machine gun-holder got in the driver's seat and the big man hopped in the passenger seat. In less than thirty seconds the van was overtaken and sped out of the underground parking.

"Uncuff him, bitch!" the masked man ordered, pointing a gun at Davis.

The older man fumbled with his keys, trying to keep his balance as the van sped through traffic. When he was able to gather himself, he uncuffed Buck Wild's leg restraints, then his hands. As soon as the cuffs fell to the floor, Buck Wild began beating the old man. The transport-jackers didn't seem to notice or care about the violence taking place a few inches away. When the prison guard no longer moved, Buck Wild let out a savage scream, his fists and arms covered in the blood of his kill.

"Woo! Hell yeah! I can't believe this shit! I'm free! Gimme one of dem guns!"

"We ain't free yet," the man said, throwing Buck Wild a change of clothes. "Put these on. We 'bout to change cars."

"Who the fuck is y'all? Where my brotha at?" Buck asked, stripping from the prison uniform and putting on the black jeans and black t-shirt.

"We on our way to him," the driver spoke up, stopping under a bridge. A white Cadillac truck was waiting. Princess sat in the driver's seat. When the escape team climbed in, the white Escalade sped away.

"He remind me of you, baby," Queenie told Pop Somethin' as she took off her mask.

When Buck Wild seen one of the people that broke him out was a woman, he couldn't hold in his surprise. Seeing her twin driving put him over the edge. "What the fuck? Y'all on some Ocean's Eight shit!"

"They got more heart than you do, nigga," Pop said, taking off his mask.

Shock and awe shown on Buck Wild's face when he looked at Pop Somethin'. Then anger. "If you didn't have that gun, I'd beat cho ass, nigga."

Pop sat the pistol on the dashboard. "Last time we went toe-to-toe, you lost, dawg."

Buck Wild clenched his fists and flexed his muscles. "I won the one before that."

"Cause you had help, nigga. It took four of y'all. I'm immortal, nigga. God ain't made a nigga that can see me one-on-one."

"Y'all ain't 'bout to start fightin' while we trynna get away?" Queenie asked, looking back and forth from Pop to Buck Wild.

"Nah," Pop waved. "Buck Wild know better. We the reason he free."

Hearing the word 'free' seemed to calm Buck Wild down and lighten the hostility. Then he began laughing. "Damn, Pop. I knew you was a beast out here, but I never imagined you would be the one to get me out."

"Life is a bitch, and fate is her sister," Pop said, repeating the line he heard from Born Ready. "You smoke, right?"

"Hell yeah!" Buck yelled, grabbing the blunt Pop handed him. "Who truck is this? This muthafucka fuckin' shit up! And y'all twins? Which one can I get, Pop?"

"You can't handle them, nigga," Pop laughed. "They a rare breed and don't fuck wit' typical niggas."

"I just did ten years, nigga. Ain't a bitch out here that can handle me!" Buck bragged before turning to Queenie. "'Sup, baby? You wearin' the fuck outta them black yoga pants.

A Gangster's Code 2

Got a nigga wantin' to know if you got some room in there for me."

Queenie gave him a sideways look. "What Pop just say? You can't handle me, nigga. Plus, Pop is my nigga. I know all about what happened in there, how he fucked you up. What I look like givin' you some pussy when you and my nigga had a issue?"

Buck sucked the back of his teeth, mugging Queenie. "That nigga wasn't on shit. But what up wit' cho sista, though? Y'all twins, right?"

"Yep," Princess spoke up from the driver's seat. "And we share everything. You big and sexy, but it's loyalty first."

It took a couple seconds for her words to make sense. When they did, Buck Wild turned to Pop Somethin'. "You fuckin' twins, brah? Real shit?"

"Rare breed," Pop grinned.

Buck Wild sat back in the seat, puffing the blunt hard. "Damn, Pop. I didn't know you had all this in you. Niggas talked about you like you was a legend, but actually seein' this shit is a trip. I heard some shit about you and C-Note soft ass out here fuckin' wit' a cartel. What up wit' that?"

"Who told you that?"

"C'mon, brah. You know niggas in the joint gossip like hos about what they heard niggas out here doin'."

"Yeah. It was some truth to that, but C-Note turned bitch and fucked it up. I'm fuckin' wit' cho brotha on this takeover."

"I knew C-Note was a bitch. That's why I pressed him like that. I hope you buried his bitch-ass."

"He got judged."

"Good. And good lookin' on gettin' a nigga out. I thought I was gon' spend the rest of my life in that bitch. Damn, I owe you, brah."

"Don't trip. This all part of the plan. Now, let's focus on gettin' this money in Atlanta."

J-Blunt

"I love the sound of that," Buck Wild smiled. "But on some otha shit, why don't you let me get a couple minutes wit' one of yo' bitches? I just did a dime. Watchin' the way shorty handle that AR and how she look in them pants got a nigga weak in the knees."

Pop looked at Queenie. "It's on you. If I was fuckin' my hand for ten, I'd be on the same shit."

Queenie tried to read Pop's face as they had a brief stare down. Deep down inside, she felt some type of way that Pop had consented to her fucking another man. She searched his face for a sign of jealously or any type of emotion that would make her decision, but Pop's face was flat. The decision was all her's, and her desire to show she was down for whatever Pop wanted won. "Okay. Just because you want me to," she said, moving to sit next to Buck. "Don't be fallin' in love wit' me, nigga. This just a fuck. I'm only doin' this 'cause I'm a real bitch and I'm showin' you some love."

Pop took the blunt from Buck Wild and moved to the passenger seat, giving them room. When Queenie sat on Buck's lap, he pulled her face to him, sticking his tongue down her throat and palming her ass. Even though he was a terrible kisser, Queenie hung in there and ground her pussy on his lap. When she felt his dick get hard, she dug in his pants to get a feel. Her body went stiff, jaw dropped, and eyes popped as she felt up his dick. His thickness and length seemed unreal. And then she felt the knots and lumps near the head.

"What the fuck is that?" she asked, snatching her hand from his pants and jumping up.

Buck grinned lustfully. "The biggest dick you eva felt in yo' life, gurl!"

Queenie stayed where she was. "Lemme see."

Buck Wild lifted enough to pull his pants and underwear down. The Louisville Slugger-sized monster dick sprang out, the lumps on it making it look like a deformed snake.

"What the fuck is that?" Queenie screamed, moving closer to Pop Somethin'.

The fear in her voice got Pop and Princess's attention. When Pop seen what had caused her reaction, he pointed a pistol at Buck Wild. "Put that nasty-ass shit up, nigga!"

***

When he walked into the apartment, Born Ready and Buck Wild hugged aggressively, then stepped back to look at each other. After smiles, they hugged again.

"Damn, boy! You big as fuck!" Born Ready said, looking his little brother from head to toe again.

"You know how it is in there. You gotta be a wolf. But what's up wit' this bald head shit? Lookin' like that nigga, Taye Diggs!" Buck Wild laughed.

"Fuck you, nigga," Born Ready laughed. "I want you to meet my lady friend, Sasha. It's because of her all this shit is about to happen."

The silver-haired BBW sat on the couch in a way-too-small pink robe with one leg crossed over the other, showing all of her naked thighs. "Welcome home, baby brother!" she smiled, standing and hugging the prison breakee.

"And this is her friend, Treazur," Born Ready introduced, pointing to the white woman who stood with Sasha.

"Welcome home, Buck Wild!" she smiled, giving him a hug.

The big man eyed the tan-skinned white woman lustfully. Her hair was braided in two long cornrows, and she wore light makeup with plenty of lip gloss. With blue eyes, a sharp nose, and high cheekbones, she flexed her curves in a blue tank top, white jeans, and heels.

"Damn, you bad!" Buck Wild grinned.

"And I'm all yours," she smiled lustfully.

Buck Wild's eyes popped as he looked back and forth from Treazur to Born Ready and Sasha. They gave approving nods. "Where my room at?" Buck asked, grabbing her by the hand.

"Second door on the left," Born Ready pointed.

Buck Wild dragged the woman down the hall like she was a sex doll instead of a human being. "I'ma grab the wheelchair from the closet. She gon' need it," Born Ready said.

Curiosity and worry shown on Sasha's face. "Is she really gon' need that? I ain't neva heard of a nigga fuckin' a bitch 'til she can't walk. Ain't no nigga dick game that good or that big."

Born Ready gave her a look as he rolled the wheelchair down the hall. "It's just some shit you don't want to see. She 'bout to earn that two hunnit."

An ear-piercing scream from behind the door made Sasha flinch. "What the fuck is he doin' to her?"

"Fuckin' her."

The screams that came from the room didn't sound like someone having sex. More like someone being tortured. Treazur's screams began high-pitched, eventually fading to hoarse, animalistic roars, then cries for help.

Sasha looked worried. "C'mon, baby. I think she need help."

"I told her about him before she took the money. She said he could get two hours. It's only been twenty minutes."

"But she screamin' for help, babe. I'm goin' in there. It sound like he killin' her."

Sasha got up from the couch, and Born Ready followed her down the hall. When they opened the door, neither of them was prepared for what they seen. Blood was everywhere, on the walls, the floor, the bed, and all over their bodies. Treazur lay on her back in blood, both of her hands locked around Buck Wild's wrist, her face blue and purple. Buck Wild was on top of her, choking her with one arm, the

86

other arm folding her leg on his shoulder as he pounded her pussy.

"Stop him! He 'bout to kill her!" Sasha screamed.

"Chill, brah! You 'bout to kill her!" Born Ready yelled.

Buck Wild acted as if he didn't hear them, lost in a sadistic zone of pleasure and pain. When Born Ready seen his brother wasn't going to stop, he ran over and pushed him off the half-dead white woman. "Fuck wrong wit' chu, nigga?"

Buck Wild blinked a couple times like he was coming back to reality. "I-I don't know what happened, brah. I blacked out."

Treazur lay on the bed choking, unable to move, covered in blood.

Chapter 9

Lithonia, Georgia was located about 20 miles southeast of Atlanta. The occupants of the small town were some of the richest people in Georgia. Lavish mansions, condos, and estates made up most of the housing market. The price tag on the cars that roamed the streets averaged $100,000. On Evans Mill Road was a row of massive, very expensive homes known as the Belair Estates. An iron gate separated the outsiders from luxurious living, and next to the big, fancy gate was a small door.

A figure dressed in black blended in with the darkness as he moved through the door quickly and quietly. At 11:00 PM on an overcast night, there were no stars or moon lighting the sky. A mile from the gate was a 4,000 square foot mansion. Big windows covered the house. When the curtains were drawn back, marble floors, expensive furniture, and rare art was shown off. But tonight the curtains were closed, and the man in black didn't care about interior decorating.

Inside the mansion, The Weeknd's voice crooned through expensive speakers. A loud sniff cut through The Weeknd's lyrics as Boss dropped the $100 bill onto the plate filled with cocaine. He brushed his nose with his index and thumb, taking several sharp sniffs. "Oh, hell yeah!" *Sniff, sniff.* "That's what I's talkin' 'bout!"

Boss was a yellow-skinned, slim nigga with close-cropped curly hair. In Atlanta, he was big fish, third in command in S.O.D, short for Stacks on Deck. The light-skinned mulatto had a thing for dark-skinned women. *The blacker the berry, the sweeter the juice* was his favorite saying, and next to him was the blackest, sweetest berry. He couldn't wait to peel off her pink bra and thong to savor the taste of her sweet fruits. "G'on, getcha some o' that," he said, passing the plate of cocaine to his guest.

The woman took the plate, grabbing the c-note in her manicured hand. A long line of cocaine disappeared when she ran the currency over the powder. After setting the plate on the back of the tub, she grabbed a shot glass of Remy and downed it.

"Yeah! That's how you do that shit!" Boss encouraged.

"Oh, yeah, baby! That's that good shit!" she moaned as the cocaine raced through her brain.

"Now, scoot on closer to yo' boy and let me finish tellin' you my plans on startin' a porno company," he said, opening his arm and motioning for her to snuggle up.

"And you sayin' I can star in yo' first movie? How much you payin'?" Queenie asked, sliding next to him and running a hand over his chest.

"Five hunnit for three scenes."

"I don't know. I mean, I wanna do it, but I gotta talk to my man about it first."

"Why? You a grown woman. Do you. This about a career."

"But he gon' eventually see it. I mean, he ain't no hater. He know I be chasin' coins. He the one that told me to get it by any means."

Boss looked surprised. "Oh. So he cool wit' chu fuckin' otha niggas?"

"As long as it ain't for free, yeah. It's all about getting the job done. He understand."

"Damn, shawty. What kinda nigga you got? I mean, don't get me wrong, I wanna fuck. You sexy and thick. But if you was my bitch, ain't no way I be lettin' you fuck these dirty-ass niggas out here. I know y'all trynna get a bag, but it gotta be limits on what you do to get it, especially if you got a nigga you love and who love you. You sure this nigga got yo' best interest in mind? 'Cause it don't sound like it. Sound like gettin' money more important than you. You fuck wit' me and you don't even gotta do this porno shit. I'll make sure you good."

90

A Gangster's Code 2

The words hit Queenie harder than she allowed to show. She thought back to the look on Pop's face when he told her she could fuck Buck Wild. He was only a few feet away, but didn't care about her giving her pussy to his enemy.

"You good?" Boss asked, noticing the look on her face.

Queenie snapped back to the moment and mission. "Yeah. What you said made me think. But I need the money. What kinda scenes is you talkin' 'bout. Describe 'em."

Boss eyed her tattooed black skin and perky breasts before running a hand over her curves. "Shit, we would start off in my Jacuzzi, like we is now. Have you come over to my bed where I would be waitin'. You tell me how horny you is and how bad you wanna suck my dick. Then you gimme some sloppy toppy. After I bust in yo' face, lemme fuck you in yo' pussy and ass."

Queenie looked unsure. "I don't know. I never did a porno."

Boss knew he had her where he wanted. All he had to do was drive a little harder. "It ain't nothin' but fuckin' on camera. Tell you what, I'ma give you eight hunnit and a Gucci bag. What you wanna do?"

The extra pay made Queenie's eyes light up. "Shit, we can do that right now. You got a camera?"

"Hell yeah! I'ma go get it!" he said, getting out of the water before she could change her mind.

"You got some chocolate or honey?" Queenie asked.

Glee passed over Boss's face when he realized what they could do with the sweet condiments. "Yeah. Go downstairs and look in the ice box."

This was Queenie's third time in the house, so she found the kitchen easily, but she bypassed the fridge and went to the back door. Pop Somethin' walked in wearing a serious look.

"Where he at?"

"Upstairs, settin' up the camera for our porno," she grinned.

When the bedroom door opened, Boss was setting the camera on a tri-pod, angling it toward the bed. "Where that chocolate sauce? You didn't find it?"

"Nope. But I found him," she said, opening the door wider.

When Boss seen Pop Somethin', instant fear gripped his body. The size of him along with his powerful aura made him seem supernatural, like he had mutant powers. When Boss seen the big, black Desert Eagle in his fist, a fart escaped his body.

"Where it at, nigga? You know what up," Pop barked.

"C'mon, brah. I don't got no–"

Fifteen feet separated the lion from his prey. Pop closed the distance in a millisecond, backhanding the half-naked man across the face with the 50 caliber hand cannon. Boss crashed to the floor and Pop stood over him, pointing the gun in his face. "Lie to me again, nigga, and you gon' die."

Boss lay on the floor trembling, holding the left side of his bleeding face. "Behind the El Chapo picture."

Pop and Queenie's eyes found the picture at the same time. Near the bed was a framed poster of the Mexican drug lord. After a nod from her nigga, she covered her hands with the bed sheet and removed the frame. Behind it was a medium-sized wall safe.

"What's the combo?" Pop demanded.

"9-05-02."

Queenie punched in the numbers. When she felt the door unlock, she nodded to Pop. The Desert Eagle coughed, sending a bullet exploding into Boss's face. The back of his skull opened when the metal slug burst through brains and bone. Pop walked over to examine his handiwork and noticed the red light on the camera. "Damn. He recordin' us."

"Freaky-ass nigga was ready," Queenie laughed.

A Gangster's Code 2

"Anything in there?" Pop asked, pulling the flash drive from the camera.

Queenie pulled out seven stacks of banded bills, two iced-out watches, and a diamond-encrusted chain. "I like Atlanta already," she smiled.

"Fuck wit' cho boy. I told y'all this was a good move. How much money in those stacks."

"It look like ten thousand. Damn, baby. Every move you made since I been wit' you been the right one. I'm wit' chu, baby, all the way to the end," Queenie expressed. She wanted to say more, but didn't. Now wasn't the time.

Pop noticed her reaction. "You got somethin' else to say?"

"Nah. Not really. But somethin' Boss said made me wonder how you feel about love."

Pop gave her a look. "It's a dead nigga on the floor and I got a video of it in my hand. You holdin' the bag. Why the fuck is you thinkin' 'bout love when we makin' moves?"

"Because he just said it. And I been thinkin' 'bout it a lot lately. And this powder got me trippin'."

Pop walked over and grabbed the money and jewelry. "Get dressed so we can get the fuck outta here."

Pop's gait was fluid, his strides long and purposeful. Queenie struggled to keep up with him, happy she put the running shoes in her bag. They had been walking for close to five minutes, neither of them speaking. A few minutes later the gate came into view. Their getaway car was on the other side. Thoughts of a mission completed gave Queenie the courage needed to ask the question that had been burning a hole in her mind. "How do you feel about love?"

Pop cut his eyes at her and let out a deep breath. "It's the most powerful emotion we got. And it can make you weak. Make you see shit that ain't there and have you doin' shit you know you shouldn't be doin'. That shit can blind you and fuck wit' cho emotions. Somethin' that strong, I don't want no part."

"Damn, Pop. You make it seem like love is a bad thing."

"Didn't you just hear what I said? It is a bad thing, which is why I'ma stay away from it."

"But what about the lovin' families wit' parents who love they kids? What about the people who been married for ten or twenty years? The Obamas. Jay-Z and Beyoncé. Having black love. I want that with you."

Pop huffed and puffed. "Stop, Queenie. That fairytale ain't for me. Or for us. We out here trynna run it up. Can't be worried about love and kids doin' what we doin'. That shit gon' make us slip. I want a million dollars and to go back home. That love shit wasn't never in my plans."

"So you don't think or dream about it?"

"Nope," Pop answered flatly.

Queenie studied his face. He clenched his jaw several times and wouldn't look at her. Queenie had never caught Pop in a lie until now. "Why not? What happened?"

Pop took his time answering. "My uncle Ro, Shanice daddy, died because of that shit."

Queenie looked surprised. "When? How?"

"When I came from Jamaica, Ro took me under his wing and eventually introduced me to the jack game. I was still a shorty, but we was hittin' niggas. That's how he kept food on the table. What my Aunty Dorothy didn't know was Uncle Ro had a side bitch, and the side bitch had a main nigga. Ro started fallin' in love wit' her and wanted her to leave her nigga. She wouldn't, so one day my uncle got drunk and got in his feelin's. We went over the bitch house unannounced and her nigga was there. I was sittin' in the car when the nigga answered the door. Him and my uncle got to arguin', and before I could get out the car, the nigga pulled out a gun. My uncle tried to run, and he shot him in the back. I was so shocked I froze. When the police came, the nigga said my uncle tried to rob him. And even though my uncle had bullets in his back, they believed that nigga because my uncle was a known jacker."

"Damn, Pop. That's fucked up."

"I know. Which is why that love shit ain't for me. I got love for you, Queenie, but not the way you love me. Princess, too. Y'all my partners. My bitches. I ride for y'all. But all that romance and black love shit ain't for us. I wanna check a bag and fall back and live a good life. You and Princess wanna come wit' me. Cool. We a team. But if you ever wanna find that black love shit, I won't stop you. I understand what you want, and I won't ever stand in the way of that. Just don't expect me to get down on one knee."

"See, it's not that easy for me, Pop. I never felt like this before. I can't just leave. I'm in this 'til forever. I don't want nothin' wit' nobody else. I only want you, Pop. And whatever it takes to stay by yo' side, I'ma do it. I love you, and I'm in love wit' chu. You got my whole heart, and ain't no room for nobody else."

"How you feel is cool, and I'm glad you told me, but I don't feel the same. All I want is loyalty, Queenie. Nothin' more. Nothin' less."

"Do you love Shanice?"

A scowl crossed over Pop's face as he looked over at Queenie. "Why you ask me that? That's my cousin. Yeah, I do."

"But do you think about her as more than a cousin?"

Pop's body temperature rose along with his anger. "Fuck type of question is that?"

"I don't think it's nothin' wrong wit' it. I mean, look at me and Princess. But I just want to know. You had a dream about her a while ago. You was fuckin' the mattress an sayin' her name."

"We ain't finna do this, Queenie. Not now. Not ever. That's my li'l cousin. I love her like a sister. You my bitch, and I want you to stay my bitch for as long as you want. All that extra shit ain't for us. That's all I got to say about this love shit. Text Princess and see what she got."

Queenie decided to leave well enough alone. He expressed how he felt, and that was enough. For now.

***

Gus Johnson was the man in Atlanta. He stood 6'8" and was long and lean. His style of dress screamed 'Look at me, nigga! I got money!' Ice cubes in his ears, designer gold-rimmed frames on his face, an icy chain and watch, and Billionaire Mafia clothes from head to toe. Gus also had a warm and inviting demeanor and the smile of a movie star. And since he was a local celebrity from his high school hoop days, everybody in the state of Georgia knew him. That was both a good and bad thing. Bad because privacy was a luxury he hadn't known since middle school since there was always somebody watching. The good part of his celebrity was the connections. Because of his status, everybody wanted to be around him. Put the right people in the right places and magic happens, like it did when he met his partners and co-founded S.O.D. In five years the clique of drug dealers had morphed into an organization that owned businesses, real estate, and controlled almost half the drug trade in Georgia.

"B-Real, you ain't neva seen nuttin' like this!" Gus yelled from the fluffy mink pillow of the gold cabana being carried on the shoulders of twelve women. He had hand-selected the women from a local modeling agency, all of them fine enough to turn heads when they walked in a room. But put them in gold two-piece bikinis and gold body paint with Egyptian symbols drawn on their skin and they got what Gus hoped for. All eyes on him!

"Head honcho, my nigga!" B-Real called. "All rise! Stacks on Deck!" To show his point, B-Real dug into a Coach backpack filled with singles and threw them in the air before the cabana like he was throwing rice at a wedding.

A Gangster's Code 2

Wettest was the hottest club in Atlanta. Professional athletes, rap stars, pimps, and drug dealers frequented the party atmosphere to have a good time. And by showing up on a gold cabana being carried on the shoulders of twelve women dressed in gold, Gus put everyone on notice that the party was about to begin. He and the entourage were led to a large roped-off section of the club. After climbing down from the bed, Gus began greeting the party-goers, exchanging daps, hugs, and pictures with everybody who was somebody. Champagne flowed like it was water.

Another member of Stacks on Deck was in the crowd. He was just as important as Gus, if not more, but he had long ago learned being in the background had its advantages. Mecca had been in the state of Georgia for ten years. For most of that time he lived and experienced the best life had to offer. Fuckin' bad bitches, living in mansions, exotic cars, trips out of the country, enough jewelry to make a rapper jealous. Short and chubby with a small potbelly, Mecca didn't have the intimidating or charismatic features of the leader of a drug organization. His receding hairline and dark skin made him a CeeLo Green look-alike. Mecca knew he wasn't handsome or physically imposing and he probably wouldn't win many fist fights, but what he did possess was an ability to work numbers and make them grow. He came to Atlanta with sixty thousand in cash and ten kilos. Today he was a millionaire and did what he wanted when he wanted and how he wanted. And if he ever needed something done, thousands of people would kill to do his bidding.

"Where the fuck is Boss?" Gus asked as the men exchanged hugs.

"I don't know. He said somethin' 'bout a porno bitch he was fuckin' wit'. Nigga think wit' his dick too much. But he prolly show up before we leave. And I see you tried to outdo yo' last club entrance," Mecca said, eyeing the twelve gold women.

J-Blunt

Gus took a drink from a bottle of Aces before speaking. "Comin' in wit' a marchin' band was a'ight, but you know how I do. I'm over the top. Next time I come, I think I'ma walk in wit' some Komodo Dragons or sumthin'. Won't I fuck they heads up wit' that?"

Mecca laughed. "You too much, dawg. Way too much."

On the other side of the club, mixed in with the party-goers who didn't have VIP access, were Born Ready and Buck Wild. They wore dark clothes, no jewelry, and in the parking lot was a black Buick LeSabre. Tonight their goal was to see everything without being seen. And even though Buck Wild had a looming presence, nobody seemed to notice him. All eyes were on S.O.D.

"I wanna rush that nigga and squeeze off so bad!" Buck Wild groaned, the eagerness to do violence sounding in his voice.

"We gon' get what we got comin' to us, li'l brah," Born Ready said coolly, watching Mecca sip champagne and live the life.

"I can't believe that nigga ain't reach back. All this time he been out here runnin' it up."

"Don't look at it like that. It's all about perspective. Nig-ga been out here gettin' it up so he can put us on. All this is for us," Born Ready smiled.

Princess sat at the bar sipping a watery drink, looking bored. A text on the phone got her attention. It was Queenie letting her know their job was done and they were on their way to the club. Pop also wanted an update, so Princess typed back that she was still waiting to make contact. After slipping the phone in her purse, she went back to nursing the drink. Then a man approached the bar to her left.

"We need a hunnit bottles in the VIP. S.O.D."

Princess turned to see who ordered thousands of dollars worth of liquor and got a wink from B-Real. He was a little man, 5'5", slim build, low hair cut, dark skin, designer glass-es, and a diamond studded S.O.D. chain around his neck.

98

"Why you over here lookin' like you don't wanna be here?"

"'Cause I don't."

"It can't be that bad, baby."

"And if it is?"

"Then I would say come party wit' us and forget about cho problems for a night. S.O.D. in VIP. You invited. I'm B-Real. What's yo' name?"

J-Blunt

Chapter 10

When S.O.D. partied, the party never ended at the club. From Wetness, an expensive motorcade of luxury vehicles drove to a Mansion in Buckhead. All of the people that partied with S.O.D. in the club didn't come back to the mansion. Only S.O.D. members, a few sports stars with their entourage, and women were invited. In total, close to forty people partied at the after party. Pills, weed, coke, and liquor was in excess. The party didn't slow until after 5:00 AM. Mecca wasn't the type to sleep in a strange place or in a house full of strangers. After a few words with Gus, both men grabbed a groupie and left.

"Yeah, nigga. Drop me off at the honeycomb hideout. I'ma hit you when I wake up so we can get that paperwork from the coffee shop," Gus said as they walked toward the white Bentley with their groupies.

"Yessir! You think I'ma forget about anything that gotta do wit' money?" Mecca laughed.

"I hope not. I–"

Gus stopped talking when a big man dressed in dark clothes appeared from his Bentley. The shirt he wore was well-fitted, showing a powerful physique, the bald head and scarred face intimidating. Considering his physical presence, the gun in his hand was unnecessary. Next to him was a man six inches shorter and three shades darker. He was also bald headed and possessed and intimidating stare. Even though it had been ten years since they'd last seen each other, Mecca knew the pair instantly.

"This a nice car, Mecca," Born Ready spoke.

"Born Ready! What up? When you get out?" Mecca asked, visibly shaking in his shoes.

"Couple months ago. Thought I would come and holla. I hear you doin' good, and now I see this snow-white Bentley, I agree. You fuckin' it up in the ATL."

"I-I'm a'ight."

"Aye, brah, I don't know what y'all on, but we S.O.D. Stacks on Deck. What's wit' the iron?" Gus asked.

"How 'bout we get in this Bentley and find out?" Born Ready suggested.

"We don't got nothin' to do wit' this. Can we leave?" one of the women asked.

"Nah, nah. Y'all stay. Y'all in a privileged position to learn somethin'. Keep yo' eyes open."

Gus watched Born Ready and Buck Wild intently, waiting for the opportunity to make a move. He had a pistol in his waist and there were about fifteen S.O.D. members in the house one hundred feet away.

Born Ready noticed the look on Gus's face and sensed his eagerness to make a move. "You a'ight, brah?" Born Ready asked, pulling a pistol from his waist.

"Yeah, brah. I'm good."

"You ain't 'bout to die trynna be a hero, is you?"

The men locked eyes, feeling each other out. During the stare, Gus realized Born Ready knew his thoughts. When Gus could no longer hold the intuitive man's stare, he looked away.

"Now that we got that out the way, ladies, I need y'all to search these niggas for guns and cell phones, and then we can get on our way," Born Ready said.

After getting the phones and guns, Mecca drove, Born Ready took the passenger seat, and Gus, Buck Wild, and the women hopped in the back.

"Why you doin' this, brah? What you want?" Mecca asked.

"What we got comin', nigga. You been out here fuckin' it up while me and li'l brah was fucked up. That was my move. You took our shit and never sent it. What you got for us?"

"Y'all don't need guns for that. My nigga, I got a hunnit Gs for both y'all."

The number impressed Buck Wild. Born Ready looked unfazed. "I heard y'all worth Ms, Mecca. Millions. That's what I need."

"Okay, okay. Um, I can't just go to bank and take that kinda money out. You gotta gimme some time."

"You got about five seconds to tell me where the dope and money stash is. I ain't stupid, nigga, so don't insult my intelligence."

Mecca paused to think over Born Ready's words. He needed a way to stall. "That shit on the highways right now. I won't be able to get my hands on that for 'bout a week.

Born Ready looked in the back seat and pointed at both women. Buck Wild shot them in the face.

"Oh shit!" Gus screamed, wiping the dead women's blood from his face as one of them fell into him.

"Next bullet got cho boy name on it," Born Ready said calmly. "We need that stash, Mecca."

"Okay, brah! Okay. You got it."

"Where we goin' and how many people in the house?"

"Westside. Got a stash house."

"What's in there?"

"'Bout a half mil. Twenty or thirty bricks."

Born Ready smiled. "That's a good start."

Nobody noticed Gus's hand sliding to the door handle. After stopping at a red light, the Bentley slid across the intersection, picking up speed. Gus pulled the tab, quickly unlocking the door. The distinct clucking sound of the lock being disengaged caused his captors' heads to jerk in his direction, but Gus moved swiftly. As he dove from the car, Buck Wild tried to grab him, not only came away with a ripped piece of his shirt.

Born Ready began laughing. "Stupid-ass nigga!"

***

Gus rolled to a stop in the middle of the street, the adrenaline rushing through his body blocking the pain from jumping out of a car going thirty miles an hour. The headlamps of a dark-colored Buick came to a stop a few feet from him.

"Help! I just got kidnapped!" Gus screamed, running toward the car.

The passenger door opened and B-Real stepped out. When Gus seen his boy, relief washed over him. "B-Real, they kidnapped Mecca! They on they way to the brick lair!"

Alarm and surprise showed on B-Real's face. "Oh shit! C'mon, brah. Get in."

Gus moved to the rear passenger door. When it opened, the first thing he noticed was the dark-skinned woman with dreadlocks pointing a gun at him. The second was the big, dreadlocked man sitting next to her. When he looked in the driver's seat and seen the identical twin of the woman in the back seat, he turned to B-Real.

"S.O.D., brah. We day-one. This how you do us?"

"We under new management."

The pain of betrayal on Gus's face was too much for B-Real. As soon as he looked away, Queenie began squeezing the trigger. The loud pops and sounds of bullets digging into flesh made B-Real look up again. Gus lay in the street, blood gushing from lethal wounds to his neck and chest. The look on the dying man's face said more than any words could. Tears filled B-Real's eyes as he watched the man he once loved like a brother die slowly.

"Let's go, nigga!" Pop called from the back seat, interrupting the moment shared by B-Real and his dying friend.

After wiping the tears from his eyes, B-Real got back in the Buick. A short drive later, Princess parked behind the Bentley outside a big, white house.

A Gangster's Code 2

Pop got the women's attention. "Y'all stay out here. Send me a text if y'all see somethin'. C'mon, B-Real."

Born Ready, Buck Wild, and Mecca had already gotten out of the Bentley. When Pop walked up with B-Real, Mecca's eyes got wide as the sun. "You did this!" he accused.

"They made me an offer I couldn't refuse. I'm the face of Stacks on Deck now."

"You bitch-ass, Judas-ass nigga! Fuck-nigga!" Mecca cursed, wishing he could get his hands on his betrayer.

"Y'all discuss that later," Born Ready interrupted. "Take us in the house."

The Brick Lair had a top-notch security system with cameras, lights, and alarms. The doors were specially designed to withstand the force of battering rams and any attempts to get in forcefully. Unless someone blew the door open with a bomb, there was no getting in the Brick Lair.

But the crew from Texas didn't need a bomb. They had Mecca and B-Real. After sending an emergency text to the sole occupant in the house, the five men approached the door. When it opened, a wild-looking Haitian man showed himself.

"What up, Mecca?"

"Let us in. Lock the door behind us."

When everybody was inside, Solo locked the door. He turned and seen Pop Somethin', Buck Wild, and Born Ready brandishing weapons.

"A'ight, ch'all," Born Ready spoke up. "Show us the money!"

Solo was surprised by the guns. He looked to Mecca for a sign of what to do. The leader of S.O.D. shook his head and mugged B-Real. Solo caught on quick and attacked B-Real. Pop Somethin's Desert Eagle boomed, taking a chunk out of the Haitian's face.

Born Ready pushed Mecca forward. "Let's go, nigga. Time is money!"

The safe was on the second floor, and it was as big as a bedroom. After Mecca put in the combo, the locks released and the door opened. Inside the safe, shelves lined the walls. On those shelves was $600,000. There were also two tables in the middle. Seventy bricks of ninety percent pure cocaine was stacked up neatly.

The men were in awe of the drugs and money. Everyone except Mecca. He knew this was his only opportunity for escape, so while the robbers' attention was occupied, Mecca took a swing at B-Real, catching him on the chin. The betrayer seen a light flash in his brain as he fell to his knees. Mecca sprinted for the door, planning to lock the robbers in the safe. He had just stepped into the hallway when the gunfire erupted. Hot lead slammed into his back, ass, and legs, throwing off his momentum. After catching his balance, Mecca fell against the safe door, trying to close it. Pop and Buck Wild ran at the door, the big men lowering their shoulders and hitting it hard. They hit the door right before it was able to latch, their momentum and strength sending the door flying open. Mecca was lifted from his feet and thrown into a nearby wall.

"Damn, brah. Why you go and get cho'self shot?" Born Ready asked as he stood over Mecca.

"Fuck you, nigga. I knew you was gon' kill me."

"You stupid, nigga. Stupid for thinkin' you wasn't gon' see me again after takin' my shit. All you had to do was throw niggas a lifeline. Now you lost it all. B-Real took yo' spot."

"Fuck B-Real. He gon' get his. Y'all ain't gon' get away wit' this shit."

Born Ready lifted the gun to Mecca's face. "I guess you won't never know how this story end, huh?"

Chapter 11

The murders of Gus and Boss were big news in Atlanta. A month had gone by since the killings, and so far the police had no suspects, witnesses, and hundreds of unanswered questions. The million dollar question was where was Mecca? Everybody who had knowledge of S.O.D. knew there were three major figures. Two of them had been found murdered. The third was unaccounted for.

Rumors in the streets said Mecca killed his second and third in command and fled to Cuba with fifty million. Since he didn't have any roots in Georgia, most people didn't have a hard time believing the fictitious tale, but no one in S.O.D. paid any attention to the rumors on the ground. They knew Mecca to be fair, generous, and trustworthy. For those loyal members who didn't believe the worst about their leader, B-Real fed them lies, saying another clique, S.O.D.'s rival Grind Squad, was behind the hit. The bloodthirsty Stacks on Deck members believed the lie like it had come from an eyewitness.

"This shit feel like a fuckin' dream!" Buck Wild slurred, tilting the bottle of Rose to his lips and spilling most of it on his clothes.

"Yo' drunk ass!" Born Ready laughed. "I told you we was gon' do it big when you got out. I wasn't playin'."

"Dawg, we can make a movie outta this shit. Write a book or somethin'. I betcha that shit do numbas. Niggas broke me out and then we took over a city! What! I want Terry Crews to play me!" Buck laughed.

The brothers lifted their bottles of Rose and toasted, celebrating their newfound success. They were partying with S.O.D. in a strip club called SWEAT. Stacks on Deck had taken over most of the club, partying to show the city they hadn't folded at the loss of their leaders.

At the center of the S.O.D. circle was the new leader, B-Real, along with the newest S.O.D. members, Buck Wild, Born Ready, and Sasha, Born Ready's girl, who was also B-Real's cousin. They met while he was in a halfway house. Sasha worked at the same factory as Born Ready. After a few fucks, he learned she had family in Atlanta. A few more questions revealed B-Real was S.O.D. When Sasha hooked up a meeting between Born Ready and B-Real, the master chess player was able to tempt the envious backstabber with the promise of a bigger spotlight and the title of leader of S.O.D. Now they were living the new reality.

Next to the S.O.D. leader's booth was another booth. Pop Somethin', Queenie, and Princess occupied it, looking like they were also having a good time, except they sipped watery drinks and watched everything. While Pop trusted Born Ready and planned to stay in Atlanta to get his money up, he didn't trust anyone else associated with S.O.D. Which is why he didn't want to become an official S.O.D. member. Him and his bitches were more like groupies with full access.

"This seem way too easy," Queenie said, watching as S.O.D. partied like they didn't have a care in the world.

"I agree. Which is why we gotta stay on point," Pop said. "This shit can fold at any moment, which is why we gotta stay ready to go. We ain't makin' no home like we did in Dallas. We can't make the same mistake."

"This shit is bold, I tell you that," Princess added. "Born Ready is a beast, baby. I don't think we should be in a rush to leave. Atlanta is a gold mine. I think we should bleed this bitch dry."

"And we will. We still gotta put phase three down. That's gon' give us the whole city, and all that gon' bring a lot of drama. I don't want us too close to S.O.D. when the war start. Born Ready smart, but he ain't givin' Grind Squad enough respect. That might be the downfall."

"That's why we gotta stay in the shadows," Queenie nodded.

A Gangster's Code 2

A loud voice interrupted Nikki Manaj's *Chun Li* playing in the club. On the main stage Buckey, SWEAT's owner, addressed the crowd. "A'ight, ch'all. What ch'all 'bout to see gon' blow y'all minds and make y'all happy y'all paid that hunnit dolla cover charge to see this. If y'all seen her movies, then y'all know she don't play. And to help her, she brought a couple friends. Without further ado, Stormy the Man Eater!"

The lights in the club dimmed as the stage lights brightened. Rihanna's *Work* played through the club's speakers as a woman walked onto the stage. Nothing about her was average. At 6'2", Stormy towered over most women. With heels, her height jumped to 6'6", and she towered over most men. The Man Eater's face was hidden by a rhinestone mask with eyeholes. Her ears, neck, wrists, and hands were also covered in rhinestone jewelry. Her body was covered with a black silk robe, but the curves were noticeable through the sheer fabric. She walked to the middle of the stage and sat on a barstool.

After beckoning to the side stage, a petite woman dressed in a skin-tight, white mini dress wheeled out a table with a number of items on it. Stormy picked up a long sword and showed it to the crowd. After licking both sides of the blade, she stood and stuck most of the sword down her throat. The crowd applauded, wanting more.

For her next trick, she picked up a cucumber the size of a toddler's arm and gave it to her assistant. After Stormy got on her knees, the assistant began pushing the giant vegetable in the Man Eater's mouth. It took a few minutes, but the cucumber eventually disappeared. The crowd applauded, awed by the amazing oral trick.

When they calmed, she took off the robe and mask, allowing the people to see the up-and-comer in the porn world. Stormy wasn't a pretty woman. She realized that way before she got her first period, but no one could resist her sex appeal. It oozed from her body when she walked, talked, or looked someone in their eyes. Peanut butter-brown skin, almond-shaped eyes and lips so big she could use a tube of lip gloss in a couple days, her body looked put together by a comic book artist. Giant, natural K-cup breasts were bigger than a grown man's head. Her stomach wasn't flat, but she wasn't fat, either. She had just enough belly to poke out a little when she had a big meal. Her hips were so wide it looked like she had to walk through a door sideways, thighs big and meaty. Her ass was in the world record book for the biggest natural ass in the United States. When she danced for the club, niggas went crazy, thunderstorming money on the stage.

After turning the crowd up, she lay on her back and showed how flexible she was by locking her legs behind her neck. Her assistant came out again and handed her the cucumber and a bottle of Grey Goose. Before using the props, the petite woman buried her face in Stormy's pussy, making the sexy amazon moan in pleasure.

When she was good and wet, the assistant grabbed the liquor bottle and cucumber and covered them in lubricant. Stormy got on her knees, facing the crowd, and the assistant began pushing the giant cucumber in her pussy. After half of it was in, the assistant began pushing the Grey Goose bottle in her ass. When both holes were packed, the Man Eater reached back and fucked herself with the cucumber while the assistant fucked her in the ass with the liquor bottle. Again, the crowd went wild and threw more money. Then Stormy addressed the crowd.

"Okay, y'all. For the last part of my show, I'ma need some help. Somebody find me the biggest, strongest nigga out there."

All eyes in the club went to the center of the S.O.D. clique. Pop Somethin' didn't want the spotlight, so he shrank in the seat. Buck Wild, on the other hand, encouraged by the liquor and a few S.O.D. members, stood.

"Ooh, yeah!" Stormy moaned. "Bring yo' sexy ass up here!"

Buck Wild stumbled through the crowd and up on the stage.

"What's yo' name, sexy?" she asked, looking at the S.O.D. member like she wanted to eat him.

"Buck Wild, baby!"

"Flex them muscles for the crowd so they can see you."

The big man began to flex and pose like he was in a body building contest. After some encouragement by Stormy and other women in the club, Buck Wild took off his shirt and posed some more. The Man Eater joined in, rubbing oil over Buck Wild's upper body.

"Okay. Now that y'all seen what Buck Wild got, lemme show y'all what I got," Stormy said. "Lady, bring me a rubber."

The assistant appeared again, moving toward Buck Wild with a big-ass condom. She grabbed his hand and began rolling the condom on all the way up to his elbow. Buck Wild looked confused until Stormy lay on the stage and opened her legs.

"Put cho fist in her," the assistant said, pouring lube onto his hand.

Silence overcame the club as they watched in anticipation. Buck Wild was a big man with hands the size of Shaquille O'Neal's. He knelt next to Stormy and made a fist.

"Wait," Stormy said, stopping him. "Put yo' hand in first and loosen me up."

Buck Wild went slowly, eventually sticking his whole hand in her pussy. After moving it around a few times, he pulled his hand out and balled it into a fist. When he pushed his knuckles into her pussy, the Man Eater moaned, grabbing his wrist and guiding his fist inside.

A few pumps later the show was over. The crowd went wild, throwing more money onto the stage. Buck got up and helped Stormy to her feet. They shared a hug, during which she reached down and grabbed his dick. When she realized he was packing a weapon in his jeans, her eyes bucked.

"Is this real?"

Buck Wild grinned. "Hell yeah! Biggest dick you eva seen."

"Lemme see."

He looked unsure, so Stormy addressed the crowd. "Listen, y'all. I ain't playin' when I say this nigga got the biggest dick I ever felt. Don't y'all wanna see me swallow it?"

The crowd went wild, everyone except Pop Somethin', Queenie, Princess, Born Ready, and Sasha. When Buck Wild heard the cheers, it went to his head and he dropped his pants. The cheers turned to gasps when they seen the monstrosity between the big man's legs. Niggas in the crowd turned away, and the women looked horrified.

However, Stormy looked like she had fallen in love. She dropped to her knees, staring at his meat like she had been hypnotized. She stroked him lovingly, her eyes wide with amazement. Then she began taking him into her mouth. At first the feat looked almost impossible. But the Man Eater was about to earn her nickname. She took him in inch-by-inch, slowly and methodically.

Although the sight was a little sickening, nobody in the crowd could turn away. They all looked on in stunned silence as the porn star showed them something they had never seen before. And when Stormy's nose and lips touched Buck Wild's pubic hair and balls, everybody in the club with money in their pockets threw it on the stage.

***

"Hey, cousin!" Sasha smiled, opening the door of her and Born Ready's townhouse and letting B-Real in.

"Shit. What up wit' chu? Where yo' nigga at? And why er'time I come over here you ain't got no clothes on?"

112

"'Cause my man don't want me to wear clothes in the house," she said, tightening the belt on her way too small pink robe. "Born Ready in the shower. He be out in a minute."

B-Real walked over and made himself at home on the couch. "Where Buck Wild fool-ass at? And why didn't nobody tell me that nigga had a dick as big as a tree?"

Sasha's eyes popped. "Wasn't that shit nasty as fuck? Ain't no way a bitch can suck and fuck that nigga. He damn near killed my friend when he got out. Bitch had to have a hysterectomy."

B-Real burst out laughing.

"That shit ain't funny, nigga. He fucked her up. I'm glad he finally got somebody that can handle his ass. I ain't rollin' no more bitches out my house in a wheelchair."

"That shit sound crazy. Where he at now?"

"Still at the hotel wit' that porno bitch."

"They a match made in heaven, huh?" he laughed. "Aye, tell me 'bout this nigga Pop Somethin'. I can't figure the nigga out. Who is he? How y'all get wit' him?"

"I don't know too much about him, just what the streets say back in Texas. They talk about the nigga like he a god or somethin'. Only nigga I ever heard that went to war wit' a cartel by hisself."

B-Real gave her an eye. "Yeah right! A cartel? By hisself?"

Sasha raised her right hand like she was swearing on a Bible in court. "That's what they say back in Houston. Right before we came to Atlanta, he killed six niggas that came by his aunty house to kill him. He the one that broke Buck Wild out. Matter of fact, he was locked up wit' Buck Wild and whooped his ass."

B-Real looked stunned. "You tellin' me this nigga did all this shit and ain't nobody touched 'im? You make the nigga sound like a superhero."

"I'm just tellin' you what I heard. The nigga ain't said more than two words to me, so I ain't asked him shit, but he for real with everything he do. And them bitches he got ain't to be fucked wit', either. Pop Somethin' is the devil, and Queenie and Princess is his demons."

***

Queenie lay on the bed, dressed in a pink panty and bra set, talking to Shanice on Facebook. "How is the baby? You been keepin' up with those doctor appointments?"

"Yeah. He's good, and I'm good. I just feel so lonely. A couple months ago I had two niggas I was in love with, plus you and Pop was close by. Now I don't got nobody."

"It's a mind thing, girl. You feel how you want to feel. And just because we not in the same state don't mean we ain't close. Ever since that day I came to yo' house and. You know. I've been carrying you in my spirit. Distance can't separate two people who care about each other."

"C'mon, Queenie," Shanice whined. "Why you gotta talk like that? That wasn't s'posed to happen."

"But it did. And I can't stop thinkin' 'bout it. Do you ever think about it?"

Shanice looked away from her phone screen. "I mean, I do. But I don't know how I feel. I'm confused. I've never kissed a woman before."

"That's okay. We have time for you to figure it out. I'm not going anywhere. I told you, I'll be there for you and the kids. I'm keepin' my word. Do you want me to come see you? Everything has settled down, and I might be able to get away for the weekend."

Shanice hesitated. "I wanna see you, but I don't know."

"What is it to know? We friends. If you feelin' lonely, I will come spend time with you."

"Okay. Yeah. Sure. When are you coming?"

A Gangster's Code 2

"I don't know. Let me check into some things. I'll call you back later."

When Queenie hung up the phone, Princess gave her a sideways look and shook her head. "You wrong for doin' that girl like that."

"She lonely and confused. I'm just trynna help out."

"No, you not. You trynna fuck her, and then you think you can use her to get close to Pop. This a bad idea, Queenie. Don't do this. Leave Shanice alone."

"But I love him, and he loves her. This the only way."

"Queenie, listen to me, sis," Princess said, staring her twin directly in the eyes. "You sound crazy. Pop is not gon' fuck his cousin and admit bein' in love wit' her. And that is not gon' make him love you. He told you he don't want love. Don't set yo'self up to get hurt."

Queenie let out a deep sigh, looking away. When she spoke again, her mind was made up. "I'm goin' to Texas this weekend. I'ma tell Pop I'm goin' to see the family. I need you to back me up, okay?"

Chapter 12

In the world of luxury cars, Maybachs were at the top of the list. And thanks to his new rank as the leader of S.O.D., B-Real's money had grown long enough to buy his dream car. As he whipped the $200,000 machine through the streets of Atlanta, he knew he had reached the top of the food chain. Every nigga wanted to be him, and all the bitches wanted to fuck him.

"I ain't feelin' them Texas niggas you brought to the team. Somethin' ain't right 'bout dem niggas. I just don't know what it is yet," Ken-Ken said. The youngster had been with S.O.D. for almost two years. Tall and skinny with a short afro and bug eyes, Ken-Ken had worked his way into B-Real's sight by his ability to think.

"You trippin', li'l brah," B-Real said, giving him a mug. "That's my family, and them niggas certified. They gon' be the reason we smash Grind Squad and take over the whole state."

"C'mon, brah. You know that shit unnecessary. That's why Mecca, Gus, and Boss never tried it. Can't get money and go to war."

B-Real got loud. "And you see what happened! Them niggas dead! Grind Squad did that shit thinkin' we was gon' fall apart. But we gon' show them niggas we still strong when we get they ass out the way."

Ken-Ken wasn't intimidated by B-Real's outburst. "I don't think Grind Squad did it, my nigga. They was gettin' money before we was. They also know we can't let nothin' like this go unpunished. Some of them niggas came to Boss and Gus funeral. I don't know, brah. I don't think it was them."

A chill went through B-Real's body. "Tell me what you think."

"I'm not sure what happened. I just think it's more than what we think. They didn't kill Boss an' 'em for the money 'cause we still gettin' it up. And why er'body talkin' 'bout Gus and Boss, what about Solo, the Haitian at the Brick Lair? He missin', too. He coulda had somethin' to do wit' all this shit, but ain't nobody even brought him up. I think we should sit back 'til we get some more info. Our next move gotta be a smart one."

B-Real took his eyes off the road to glance at his passenger. The 22-year-old was smart and knew how to think on his own. And right now, that was dangerous. B-Real didn't need niggas with the ability to think on their own stirring the pot.

"Damn, Ken-Ken. I didn't know you had a mind like that. I like the way you think, which is why I'm makin' you my underboss. I'ma keep you wit' me at all times. I need a nigga that can think like you glued to my hip."

Ken-Ken smiled like the President of the United States had just asked him to be a part of his cabinet. "A'ight. So, what all I gotta do?"

"Nothin'. Just be you and er'thang gon' work out. But hold on. Lemme make a call."

Ken-Ken listened as B-Real made a call to Born Ready. They talked briefly about phase three. After hanging up, the red Maybach made a couple stops before parking outside of Born Ready's house. Born Ready, Buck Wild, and Pop Somethin' were waiting on the porch. When the Maybach pulled up to the curb, the Texans climbed in the back seat.

"Damn!" I didn't know these muthafuckas was this big," Buck Wild commented at the way they fit easily in the back seat.

Pop Somethin' didn't speak. He was wondering why B-Real had brought a tag-along.

"Fuck he doin' here?" Born Ready asked, not holding back.

A Gangster's Code 2

"I just made Ken-Ken my new underboss," B-Real said coolly.

"You told him 'bout phase three?" he asked cautiously.

B-Real laughed. "Hell nah! I brought him wit' me 'cause we was just talkin'. The young nigga smart, and I think y'all need to hear him out." Then he turned to Ken-Ken. "Tell 'em what you told me about Grind Squad not hittin' Gus and Boss."

The clean-faced youngster spun in the seat to face the Texas killas. When he was received with hostile stares, he nodded, hoping to defuse the tension. It didn't work. Pop Somethin' and Buck Wild's faces seemed to get angrier, so he focused on Born Ready. "I think somebody else killed Boss and Gus. I don't think it was Grind Squad. They been gettin' money next to us for a long time. Why start shit now? It don't make sense. Plus, Mecca and the Haitian bodies was never found. It's too many questions. Plus, some of them Grind Squad niggas came to the funerals. They was showin' respect, not trynna disrespect us. Whoever killed Gus and Boss wanted us to think it was Grind Squad so they can get away, but that's where they fucked up at. Grind Squad got money, too. If we hit they leaders, a war gon' kick off, and ain't nobody gon' get money."

Born Ready stared at the youngster like he had just solved a geometry problem.

"Nigga sharp, ain't he?" B-Real asked.

"Yeah. Too smart. Now I see why he yo' underboss. So, tell me, Ken-Ken, how many people you talk to about these thoughts?"

"Nobody. Just y'all."

Born Ready sat between Pop Somethin' and Buck Wild. He looked back and forth to both killers. "One of y'all take care of this nigga. I left my banger at home."

The Desert Eagle was in Pop's fist in the blink of an eye.

"Wait! Wait! Wait!" B-Real screamed.

Pop gave him an irritated look. "What, nigga?"

Ken-Ken was as scared as he had ever been, and for a moment his life appeared to be saved.

"Don't shoot him in the Maybach. The seats is hand-sown. Lemme pull over."

Panic flashed on Ken-Ken's face again.

"You trippin', nigga," Born Ready laughed, turning to Buck Wild. "Get 'im, li'l brah."

The 6'4", 250-pound goon didn't hesitate. He reached over the front seat and grabbed the smaller man in a choke-hold. Ken-Ken tried to resist, but it was useless. Buck Wild pulled him into the back seat on his lap.

When Ken-Ken passed out, Buck Wild continued squeezing his throat and leaned forward, crushing his body. Loud pops sounded as the youngster's back and neck broke. Buck kept squeezing, twisting, and folding the body, stuffing him on the floor and resting his feet on top.

"Now you ain't gotta worry 'bout blood on the seat, nigga," Buck laughed.

B-Real's body shook as a chill ran through him. "Damn, that shit was vicious. Remind me not to piss you off."

Buck gave him a mug. "Don't piss me off."

"Ken-Ken got me thinkin' 'bout phase three. What if that ain't the right move? Shit is goin' good now. Why fuck that up?" B-Real asked.

"Nah. Phase three gotta happen. It's the only way to taka all the heat off us. We gotta put the bodies on somebody. We can't have niggas gettin' suspicious, like Ken-Ken. If we don't make a move, we gon' lose the whole team," Born Ready said.

"But what about the war? We ain't gon' be able to get money and war. That shit gon' put a dent in our pockets and make the whole city hot."

"You ever heard of a war of attrition?"

"A what?"

A Gangster's Code 2

"A war of attrition. It's about who can last the longest. Er'body ain't cut out for this war shit. You hit niggas in the right places and they gon' fold, just like boxin'. You seen what my niggas can do. Y'all city ain't seen nothin' like the pain we can bring. This ain't gon' be no war, B-Real. We gon' slaughter niggas. S.O.D. comin' out on top."

"I think you should consider what he sayin'," Pop spoke up, getting everyone's attention.

Buck Wild mugged Pop. Born Ready expressed the way he and his brother felt. "Fuck you talkin' 'bout, Pop?"

"He got a point. I came to Atlanta to get money, not get caught up in a war. Like he said, war fuck up a nigga bag. I think we should reconsider phase three."

Buck laughed. "I know that ain't no bitch I hear in you!"

Pop gave Buck Wild a serious stare. "I know we been around each other a lot since you came home, but that don't mean you can play wit' me like that. Don't eva mention my name and 'bitch' in the same sentence."

The smile vanished from Buck's face as he sat up straight in the seat. "Or what, nigga? I was just bullshittin' and you in yo' feelin's. I ain't no bitch either, nigga. You seen how I get down. You know what it is."

Born Ready seen the seriousness in Pop Somethin's eyes, so he spoke up to prevent a clash of street titans. "C'mon, y'all. Chill. He was just playin', Pop."

Pop Somethin' delivered his favorite line, the mug on his face matching the seriousness in his tone. "Niggas get killed for playin' too much."

Buck Wild rolled his shoulders and flexed his muscles. "You sayin' you gon' kill me, nigga?"

"I'm sayin' you betta fall back 'fore I put chu on the floor next to Ken-Ken."

Buck took a swing. The back seat of the Maybach was spacious enough for Pop to dodge the punch and throw one of his own. It landed on the bridge of Buck's nose. Born

Ready grabbed Pop's other arm to keep him from knocking his little brother out.

"Okay! Okay! A'ight, y'all. Chill," the smaller man yelled, showing his strength as he separated Pop and Buck Wild.

Buck Wild checked his nose to see if it was bleeding. Red fluid covered his knuckle. The growl that escaped his body didn't sound human. Extra blood in his muscles seemed to make him grow bigger.

"Buck! Chill, nigga! Damn!" Born Ready yelled. "We got a dead body in the car. Fuck wrong wit' chu nigga? Chill!"

Pop relaxed some of the tension in his shoulders, but kept his eyes on Buck Wild. "I'm good."

"I ain't," Buck breathed, calming himself down. They had a dead body in the car. Now wasn't the time to settle his issue with Pop Somethin'. "Before this is all said and done, I'ma fuck you over."

"Nigga, what the fuck I just say? Chill!" Born Ready snapped "We don't got time for no fuck-shit. That shit y'all had while y'all was locked up is over now. We got plans to make money. Phase three is a green light. We gon' eliminate the competition and take over."

***

"Damn, she is so fuckin' cute. And she look just like you. Every time I see her, I want a little me," Queenie said, watching Shawntale ride the merry-go-round. There was a carnival in town.

"Yeah. She is my mini-me. But I don't think my cousin ready for no kids. He still wild. Havin' a baby might make him worse. You see how he still treats me like I'm a kid. Imaging how he would treat his daughter. That would be scary."

"I know. Kids ain't for Pop. I wish he did want a family. I love his crazy ass. That's my nigga."

"Is that what you want? A family?" Shanice asked, paying extra attention to Queenie's answer.

"Yeah, but Pop don't. He don't want love. Said it makes us weak. He wants loyalty. Told me if I ever find somebody to fall in love with, he would let me go."

There was a hint of pain in Queenie's voice. Shanice felt it. "Damn. That's kinda fucked up. But at least you know how he feels. What about your sister? I know y'all live together. Do y'all, um, sleep together, too?"

Queenie gave Shanice a curious look. "Why would you ask me that?"

"I don't know. I thought I heard you or Pop say both of y'all was his bitches. I guess I wanted to know how it worked, sharing a man with your sister."

Queenie laughed. "I know what you thinkin'. It's different, but yeah, Pop is both our nigga. But Princess more like him when it comes to love. She love him, but she not in love with him. That's her nigga. He my man."

Shanice shook her head, thankful she wasn't a part of a confusing love triangle. "That sounds crazy. I couldn't picture sharing my man, especially with my sister. What if he gives her more attention? Do you get jealous?"

"I know you ain't talkin' 'bout nobody crazy love triangle," Queenie said, calling Shanice out. "You had two niggas, and you know as well as I do Nitty was fuckin' other bitches."

Shanice looked away, a busted look on her face. "Okay. You got me. I'm not innocent. But you know how it is. Nitty wasn't shit. I like C-Note."

"And me and my sister like Pop. It don't bother me that they have sex. At least I know who he doin' it wit'. Plus, I love my sister. We best friends. We shared everything our whole life."

"It still sounds different. It would take some gettin' used to."

"You would be surprised what you could get used to. What the world thinks is normal may not be what feels good to you, and vice-versa. I'm sure you have a secret. Er'body does. We just don't care if people know."

Shanice looked away, unable to deny the truth. Queenie recognized the look. "I knew you was a bad bitch, Shanice! Tell me. Tell me your secret!"

"No. Not right now. I can't say."

Queenie grabbed Shanice's arm, spinning her until they were face-to-face. "You can tell me. I promise I won't judge you. If you want, I can tell you a secret first."

When Shanice looked into Queenie's eyes, they reflected trust, compassion, and genuine interest. The lonely single mother felt a connection to the dark-skinned temptress. It was spiritual and emotional. "Okay. Tell me your secret and I'll tell you mine."

Queenie didn't hesitate. "I think I'm fallin' in love with you."

Shanice was caught off guard by the honesty. "Oh. Um. I wasn't expecting that."

"And now you know. I keep havin' dreams about you. I think you're a beautiful woman, and you have a good soul. And you are sexy. I want to be the first woman to make love to you."

Shanice's skin flushed and heart rate increased. "Damn, Queenie. Your words, gurl. I don't know how to feel about all this."

Queenie seen the words were having an effect on Shanice, so she pulled back. "I'm sorry, girl. Bein' around you just," she trailed off. "Tell me your secret. I want to hear it."

"Look, Momma! I'm riding a unicorn!" Shawntale called.

A Gangster's Code 2

Hearing the child's voice broke the connection building between the women. In that moment their surroundings became real. They were at a crowded carnival. Shanice was five months pregnant, and she wasn't attracted to women. Especially not her cousin's bitch.

After pulling her hand from Queenie's, she went to get her daughter from the ride. When they tired of the carnival, the women went to get something to eat before heading back to Shanice's house. Shawntale tired herself out with excitement and food. By the time they got home, she was sound asleep.

After putting her to bed, the grown-ups settled on the couch to watch *Girls Trip*. Halfway through the movie, Shanice got emotional.

"What happened to C-Note, Queenie? For real. What did Pop say?"

Queenie could see the pain in her newfound friend's eyes and hear it in her voice. "He won't talk about it. To nobody. You know how Pop is when he make his mind up."

Devastation washed over Shanice. "That just don't make sense. I thought they were boys. Did Pop know C-Note took the deal and was going to testify against the cartel?"

"Yeah. They tried to kill us. They blew up our house. We lost everything."

"Damn. I didn't know that."

"I know. Pop didn't tell you because he didn't want you to worry."

Shanice lay back on the couch, tears spilling from her eyes when she closed them. "I know C-Note is dead. I knew it the night he didn't come get me. What I didn't expect was for my cousin to shut me out his life. That hurts just as much as losing C-Note. I lost two people. Three counting Nitty."

Queenie sat her drink down and moved closer to Shanice, wrapping her arms around her in a comforting way. "I don't know what to say about yo' baby daddy. Pop won't talk

J-Blunt

about it, but I guess I get how you feel. He didn't come back, but you didn't lose Pop. He loves you more than you know. To be honest, the way he love you kinda make me jealous. I wish he was that overprotective of me."

Shanice looked surprised. "Jealous of me? Yeah, right. Have you seen you? Girl, I would kill for an ass and titties like those."

Queenie blushed. "Stop. Yo' ass is just fine, and after you have the baby, yo' titties gon' be bigger than mine."

Shanice laughed, wiping the tears from her cheeks. "You crazy."

"That's what I'm talkin' 'bout! Smile and laugh. You are so beautiful. Don't be sad. The baby can feel that," Queenie said, reaching out and touching Shanice's face.

The gesture was small, but Queenie's touch was enough to send butterflies through Shanice's stomach and make her lady parts tingle. "Damn, Queenie. You driving me crazy."

The seducer leaned in close. "Good, because you do the same thing to me."

When their lips met, neither woman held back. The kiss was passionate and wet and sloppy. Moans of pleasure filled the room. The taste of Queenie's mouth unlocked hidden passions within Shanice. She wanted more, to feel Queenie's soft skin pressed against hers. "Can we take off our clothes?"

They took their time undressing, admiring the shapes and curves of each other's body. Queenie's skin was dark as night, colorful tattoos covering her body, large double-D breasts, a small waist, thick thighs, and a fat ass. Pink butterfly wings were tattooed above each of Queenie's breasts. Shanice traced a finger over the body art, her fingers taking a path of their own. She rubbed and cupped Queenie's double-Ds, moving down her stomach, waist, and thighs. The soft flesh of a woman excited Shanice. Men were hard and muscled. A woman's body molded to a man. Now she had found someone's body that could mold with hers.

126

A Gangster's Code 2

Queenie allowed Shanice to explore, liking the way inexperienced hands felt, but she wanted more, so she leaned forward and found her lips again, their tongues playing games. From her lips to her neck, down her chest, stopping at her swollen breasts. A moan of pleasure escaped Shanice's lips when Queenie flipped her tongue across the sensitive, dark brown nipple. She used her tongue to show Shanice's body pleasure no man had. All the sensitive spots were stimulated, the neck, shoulder, behind the ears, breasts, elbows, hips, and inner thighs. She paused to admire her pussy, clean-shaven, no hair bumps, the reddish-brown skin soft and flawless. Her labia was juicy and slick. After a few kisses, Queenie dove in, licking and sucking. Shanice cried out as her body was lit on fire.

Every time Queenie's tongue flipped across a body part, it burned. The orgasm built quickly, bubbling inside like a volcano about to erupt. Then it happened. The floodgates opened and Shanice's body vibrated in pleasure. Wave after wave of the electric orgasm paralyzed Shanice as all of her insides dissolved and flowed from her body.

J-Blunt

Chapter 13

An orange Range Rover cruised down Peach Tree, the occupants inside in no rush to get to their destination. Behind the tinted windows, Sid lay back in the seat, puffing a blunt of lime, doing the speed limit. Sidney Banks was the co-founder of Grind Squad. Six feet tall with a slim build, dark skin, and brushed waves, he had the aura of a boss. Whenever a nigga stood in his presence, he knew he was in the company of a leader.

In the passenger seat was Duke, one of Grind Squad's shooters. A small man, just 5'6" and 150 pounds, but his vicious nature made up for his pint size. The streets knew him to be a ruthless enforcer, and he felled many men for underestimating the size of his bite.

"That shit wit' S.O.D. is a trip, ain't it?" Sid asked. "Somethin' ain't right 'bout how er'thang went down wit' dem niggas. Why ain't nobody heard nothin' 'bout Mecca? You think he killed his niggas and hit it wit' the bag?"

"Nah. Me and the nigga wasn't close, but I talked to him enough to know he loved his team. S.O.D. was Mecca baby. You don't destroy nothin' that you build. He wasn't crazy. The last time I seen him, he mentioned cleaning that money and trynna take S.O.D. legit. When a nigga talkin' like that, you don't run away wit' the bag. You clean that shit so you can get more. I think it's somethin' foul goin' on wit' they circle. One of them niggas might've tried to make a power grab."

"That would explain a lot," Duke admitted, checking his phone after it buzzed. Me-Me flashed on the screen. "What up, baby? I was wonderin' when–"

The Range Rover jerked violently when Sid smashed the brake. A black Mustang had swerved in front of them, stopping in the middle of the street. When the SUV came to a stop, a beat-up, white Pontiac Lemans rear ended it, causing the airbags to deploy. Duke's instincts were second to none. As soon as his face hit the airbag, the Tech-9 was in his fist. After movin' the safety device from view, he lifted the semi-automatic handgun. Someone had climbed out of the Mustang with a chopper, and it was about to be set off.

K-Dawg sprang from the passenger seat of the Mustang, the AK-47 erupting death into the Range Rover's windshield. The driver made jerking moves as the bullets hit home. When K-Dawg felt a burning pain on the left side of his chest, he let go of the AK's trigger. Before he could decide to fight or flee, he felt a similar pain in his left arm. The decision to run came too late. When he spun around, four bullets in his back knocked him on the ground.

The front and rear doors of the Pontiac sprang open. Two men hopped out with rifles and began spraying the truck with bullets. They fired blindly through the frame and tinted windows, aiming for the driver and passenger seats. After a volley of bullets, they walked to the driver's side to make sure Sid and Duke were dead. When the lead man opened the door, Sid was slumped in the seat. When he looked to the passenger seat, death met him at the speed of sound as Tech-9 bullets tore into his face. The second gunman to leave the Pontiac was able to get a lock on Duke. More gunfire sounded.

"Let's go, nigga!" B-Real called from the driver's seat of the Pontiac.

Born Ready didn't respond as he peeked over at Duke. The Grind Squad shooter lay against the passenger door, breathing rapidly, blood soaking his clothing. Born Ready lifted the chopper to his face. "It's a takeover, nigga. S.O.D. in the building!"

***

A Gangster's Code 2

The navy blue Ford Explorer hadn't moved in three hours. Tinted windows made it hard to see who was inside. Seeing out wasn't a problem. Detectives Marks and Steward were 12-year veterans of the APD. For 18 days they had been keeping an eye on Dennis "D.D." Davis. A couple anonymous calls had put them onto the suspected drug dealer and murderer.

"After two weeks, what does your gut say? Did D.D. put the hit on those S.O.D. boys?" Detective Marks asked, blowing a cloud of nicotine smoke out the cracked passenger window.

"If he did, he sure as hell ain't celebrating like he should be. If I wiped out my biggest competition, I would party for a week."

"How do you know he ain't in there partying right now?"

"Because ain't nobody in the house but his old lady and kid. Nobody parties with their wife for something that happened at work," Steward laughed.

"I do. When I made detective, me and Barbra went out and celebrated."

"Which is exactly why you ain't got a social life."

"Which is also why I haven't been divorced twice," Marks shot back.

Steward gave his longtime partner a smirk as the phone rang. "This is Detective Steward. Speak your piece." After listening for a few moments, his eyes lit up. "Wait! Wait! Say that again."

Marks became anxious when he seen the excitement in his partner's features. "What's goin' on?"

Steward held up a hand, continuing to listen to the caller. "Okay. I'll make a few calls and get back to you. I think we just got what we needed to crack this case wide open." When he hung up, he faced his partner. "That was Detective Horse. That was Sid's orange Range Rover that got swiss cheesed on Peach Tree."

Mark's eyes grew wide. "S.O.D. got Sid?"

"Yep. And the two guys found in the street are believed to be S.O.D. A war is about to hit our city. The bodies are going to pile up."

"So what the fuck are we doing here? Let's get over on Peach Tree and get in on the investigation."

"Not now. Those dead bodies ain't going nowhere. Something in my gut tells me D.D.'s house is going to pop off before the night is over."

Marks wanted to protest. They had been staking out the house for hours. Everything appeared normal. The action was happening on Peach Tree, and he wanted in, but having been partners for five years, he knew to trust his partner's hunches. Following Steward's gut had led them to big collars, so he put his eagerness in check and began watching the house. Then he thought he seen something move in the bushes. "You see that?"

"No, what is it?" Steward asked, following his partner's pointed finger.

"Something moved in the bushes. Look! There it is again! There are two of them. Your gut is right again. They're about to make a move on D.D.! I'm callin' it in!"

***

"Why the fuck you park so far from the house?" Buck Wild complained.

"Because they got neighbors. People record everything, and they can get a picture of the car. Stop askin' so many questions and follow me," Pop snapped.

The house they were stalking was at the cul-de-sac of an expensive neighborhood surrounded by woods. Trees and bushes covered the landscape as if the owner didn't want to make it easy for people outside to see inside. Pop stopped near a bush to check the block. A cloud of smoke came from the passenger side of a truck a few houses away.

A Gangster's Code 2

"C'mon, Pop! Let's get to it," Buck whispered eagerly.

"Hold up. It's a truck parked out here. I don't like the way this feel," Pop warned.

"What? Fuck that truck. This phase three, nigga. Born Ready and B-Real did they part. This on us."

"We gon' have to pull it anotha day. Somebody watchin' the house."

Buck Wild looked in the same direction as Pop. He seen the SUV, but the tinted windows didn't allow him to see inside. "Fuck that shit. Ain't nobody in that truck. I'm goin' in here and killin' this nigga."

Without waiting for his partner, Buck Wild went to the side of the house and tried the glass patio door. It was locked, so he grabbed a lawn chair, throwing it through the door. The loud crash got Pop's attention. He ran to the side of the house just in time to see Buck Wild disappear inside.

The disciplined goon was stuck. Buck Wild was stupid and had rushed in the house blind. They didn't know how many people were in the house, nor the rooms they were in. Pop didn't like entering anything blind. He also had a bad feeling about the truck parked a few houses away.

Instead of running inside behind Buck, Pop crept back to the front of the house to check on the blue truck. Two men in dark suits ran toward him with their guns drawn. They spotted him at the same time.

"Stay right there!" one yelled, pointing his gun.

"Freeze! Don't move!" the other yelled, taking aim.

Pop wanted to resist, but they had the drop on him. Fifty feet of open space separated him from the trained shooters. He wanted to go for the gun in his waist, but if he flinched they wouldn't miss. If he ran, they would shoot him in the back. Pop was fucked.

Gunfire inside the house made the detectives flinch and duck. That was all Pop needed to turn the tables. The Desert Eagle came out in a blur. Bullets were exchanged. Steward caught one in the chest. Marks ducked, returning fire. Pop Somethin' felt something hot slam into the right side of his chest as he turned to run. It didn't take long to realize he was shot. The old bullet wounds in his back began to itch as a similar burning filled his chest. The threat of jail kept him on his feet.

***

Buck Wild ran through the house like a mad man. He checked most of the rooms on the first level when he heard a noise come from the end of the hall. Ready to kill, Buck Wild charged into the room, firing his pistol. When the door crashed in, a little boy dove underneath the bed. Buck bent down, about to end the child's life. Gunshots outside made him pause and think of the truck parked a few houses away. Red light flashed in his mind along with visions of a prison cell. Buck forgot about the boy and tore out of the room. When he stepped into the hallway, motion in his peripheral vision made him duck.

When D.D. seen the big shadow run into the hallway, he squeezed the trigger on the shotgun. The 12-guage boomed as a foot-long fire shot out of the barrel. The slug went high, barely missing the target. The man in black continued moving down the hall toward the recreation room. D.D. cocked the gun and fired again. Buck Wild crashed through the door, the slug just missing him. Instead of trying to fight back, Buck Wild located the nearest window and jumped through it. The woods were to his left. The 12-guage coughed behind him like a fire-breathing dragon as he disappeared.

Sirens in the distance made his heart pump faster than it ever had. One hundred yards later he came to the spot where Pop had parked the car only to find it gone. Instead of waiting around, Buck Wild used his feet to get far away from the crime scene.

Pop could feel his body getting weak as he drove the Chevy Malibu through the Atlanta streets. His chest was on fire, and the blood wouldn't stop. Lightheadedness and double vision made it hard to drive. He wasn't sure how much longer he could keep conscious. Tapping into the reserves of his strength, he pulled out his phone and called Princess.

"Hey, baby. You good?"

Pop's breathing was heavy and voice weak. "Princess. I'm. I'm fucked up. I. I got shot. Call Born Ready. Tell him. Tell him. I need help."

J-Blunt

Chapter 14

"If bein' with you is wrong, I don't ever want to be right again," Shanice sang, lying in bed with Queenie, wrapped in each other's arms.

"Ain't nothin' wrong wit' what we doin'. Life is about doing what makes you feel good. That's how you really live."

"I know. I was just raised a certain way. In church, the preachers told us gay people went to hell. Scared the shit outta me and kept me from thinking about women sexually, but I always secretly thought about it."

"So, what do you think? Was the preacher right?" Queenie asked, flipping her tongue across Shanice's lips.

"I don't know or care. You remember the secret I was going to tell you at the carnival? Well, it was my fantasies about being with a woman. I always heard women knew how to do it better. When I was pregnant with Shawntale my hormones was crazy, and I used to finger myself to lesbian porn."

"Women do know how to do it better. We are more in tune with our bodies and emotions. We are more sensual and understand each other in ways a man can't. I feel connected to you."

"Me too," Shanice admitted. "I thought it was crazy at first, but listening to you is making a lot of sense. I feel you. Literally. And I've never felt this before."

"I feel the same way. Spendin' the weekend wit' chu has been amazin'. A part of me don't want to go back to Atlanta."

"Then don't."

Queenie held Shanice's stare. The need for companionship was written all over the pregnant woman's face. "I can't do my sister and Pop like that."

"But what about me? Being with you makes me feel good. I haven't thought about Nitty or C-Note since you've been here. If you leave, I'll go back to being lonely and miserable."

Queenie suppressed the grin that tried to creep onto her face. Things were moving along quicker than expected. "I don't know, Shanice. I'm starting to feel confused, too. I'm in love wit' Pop Somethin', but I'm fallin' in love with you, too. I don't know what to do. Is you sayin' you wanna be my girl? What would yo' family and friends say if they knew you was with a woman? And what about Pop?"

"I don't know. All I know is I don't want to lose you. Didn't you say Pop would let you go if you found love?"

Queenie smiled on the inside, amused at the way her pregnant lover had used the words. "Yeah, but when Pop said it, I don't think he was picturing you as the person I would fall in love with. I don't know how he would take this news."

"What are we going to do?"

"I don't think we should do anything. Yet. We're young. We're sexy and beautiful. Let's just keep doin' what we doin'. Whenever I can, I will come visit. And when the time is right, we'll figure the next move."

Shanice sighed heavily. "Yeah. I guess so. Damn, I wish you coulda been my baby daddy."

Queenie laughed, moving in for another kiss. "I can't be yo' baby daddy, but we can be each other's baby momma."

"Mm. I like the way that sounds. Okay, baby momma. Can you do that thing to me you did with your tongue last night?"

Queenie's eyes dimmed to sexy slits. "I'ma do somethin' better. I'ma kiss and lick my way down yo' body, and we gon' have a scissor orgasm."

After some kissing and licking, the women interlocked legs and came together until their pussies were touching. They began to gyrate their hips in unison. Every time their clits touched and rubbed, sparks of electricity shot through the women's bodies. They touched, caressed, and licked body parts, the new experience setting Shanice on fire. Their pussies ground hard and fast, their juices mixing. Shanice's orgasm came in a massive wave, taking her breath away. Seeing and feeling her lover's pleasure made Queenie cum a few moments later. The ladies' lips and tongues locked again.

And that's when Queenie's phone chimed. She went to answer, but Shanice grabbed her hand. "Not now."

"Wait. Lemme just see who callin'. It might be important," Queenie said, reaching for the phone. It was a text from Princess. The sexual chemistry fled the room like shadows fleeing a fire as she read the text. "No, no, no! Oh my God, no!"

Shanice sat up, alarmed by the look on Queenie's face. "What is it?"

"It's Pop. He got shot," Queenie said, calling her sister.

Shanice frowned, making sure she heard Queenie. "What? My cousin got shot?"

Hearing Shanice repeat the words broke Queenie's heart. When Princess answered, she took off. "What happened? Where is Pop?"

Princess's voice reflected the sadness. "It's bad, sis. You gotta come back to Atlanta now. He just went into surgery. They don't know if he gon' make it."

The words stabbed Queenie in the heart, forcing a cry from her lips. "No! No! I'm on my way."

"Just come home, sis. You need to be here."

"What happened to my cousin?" Shanice asked. Queenie was speechless, so Shanice took the phone. "What happened to my cousin? Who shot him?"

"Who is this? Shanice?"

"Yeah. What happened to my cousin?"

"Look, Shanice, I can't talk about this over the phone. Plus Pop don't want us talkin' to you. I'm sorry, but that's the way it is. Tell Queenie to come home."

When Princess ended the call, Queenie sprang out of the bed, grabbing her clothes and getting dressed. Shanice ran to the closet and did the same thing.

"Nah. What chu doin'?" Queenie asked.

Shanice looked at her like she was crazy. "I'm coming with you to check on my cousin."

"No, baby girl. You can't. You heard Princess. Pop don't want us talkin' to you."

Shanice got an attitude. "I don't care 'bout none of that. He might die. I'm goin' back to Atlanta with you. Only way you gon' stop me is to kill me."

The women had a stare down. Shanice didn't blink or back down. Queenie realized Pop's cousin meant business. There was no way to stop her from coming to Atlanta short of fucking her up, and Queenie didn't want to do that. She needed the relationship to grow stronger.

"Okay. Go get Shawntale ready. I'll look up the tickets."

Because of difficulties at the airport, the women didn't make it to Atlanta until the next day. During the time, Queenie kept in constant contact with Princess, getting updates on his condition. The surgery lasted five hours, during which a blood clot had formed. Now Pop was in a coma, fighting to stay alive. During the many conversations, Queenie never mentioned her tag-alongs. She knew Princess would be pissed, so she made up her mind to deal with it when she got home.

And now that she was walking up on the porch of their two-story townhouse, she began to dread the encounter with her sister.

"Princess! Where you at?" Queenie called after unlocking the door.

"I'm upstairs!"

A Gangster's Code 2

Queenie took a last glance at Shanice before leading the way. Their bedroom had been changed into a makeshift hospital room. Pop lay in bed, bare-chested, covered by a sheet. A large gauze bandage was taped to the right side of his chest. An IV was in his arm and a breathing mask over his mouth. Machines and monitors next to the bed beeped and hummed. Princess lay in bed next to Pop wearing a worried expression.

When Queenie seen her savior, lover, and nigga lying in bed on the verge of death, devastation washed through her. She ran over, kneeling next to the bed and grabbing his hand. "Pop! Pop, wake up!"

Princess was about to tell her Pop couldn't hear her, but when Shanice walked in the room holding Shawntale's hand, Princess's concern for Pop turned to anger. "What the fuck is they doin' here? What I tell you, Queenie?"

"I didn't have a choice. She wasn't gon' let me leave without her. Who shot him?"

"You know if Pop wake up and see her, he gon' be pissed! Why would you do this? I told you not to get involved with her in the first place."

"It's too late for all that," Shanice spoke up. "I'm here now, and I'm not leaving. Who shot Paul?"

Princess took turns mugging Shanice and Queenie. "Y'all so fuckin' stupid!" she breathed. "The police shot him. I think. And he shot one of them."

Shanice's eyes popped. "The police!"

"How he get into a shootout wit' the police?" Queenie asked.

"Doin' phase three. If you wasn't out on yo' bullshit, you would know. I can't believe you brought her back home."

"Acting like a bitch won't change nothin'," Shanice sassed.

Princess sat up, looking ready to attack. "You betta watch yo' mouth, bitch! I'm not talkin' to you."

Shanice let got of Shawntale's hand, freeing her own in case Princess got beside herself. "I gotcho bitch, bitch!"

"Hey! Stop!" Queenie screamed. "We don't got no time to be fightin' each other. Chill the fuck out. Princess, tell me everything. Are the police lookin' for him?"

Princess mugged Shanice a little longer before facing her sister. "I don't think so, but it's all over the news that somebody shot a detective. They don't know who, but they say Grind Squad and S.O.D. war is the reason."

"Grind Squad and S.O.D. war? What?"

"See, this why I told yo' ass not to leave. Phase three went down. Well, some of it. Pop and Buck Wild couldn't get to D.D. Buck Wild said he ran in the house to get D.D. and Pop got into a shootout with the police that was watchin' the house. The war is officially on."

"Damn, this is so fucked up," Queenie mumbled, becoming lost in her thoughts.

"Who is takin' care of Paul? Who fixed him up? He got a doctor? Why he ain't at the hospital?" Shanice asked.

Princess gave her a 'you so stupid' look. "Because his ass would be in jail if he went to a hospital. He shot the police! Duh! But S.O.D. got connections to real doctors. B-Real and Born Ready on top of everything. I'ma call them when he wake up."

"Did the doctors say how long he gon' be in a coma?"

"They don't know. He lost a lot of blood. The doctor said he should've died from the blood loss. Then he got a blood clot during that long-ass surgery, and they thought that was gon' kill him, too. But it didn't. Now it's a waiting game."

Shanice picked Shawntale up and put her on her lap as she sat on the bed. With her free hand she rubbed Pop's leg. "Damn, cousin. Wake yo' ass up. You better not die on us. You betta not."

***

A Gangster's Code 2

Two days had passed since Shanice had come to Atlanta, and Pop still hadn't woken. Doctors and nurses had stopped by, but there was no change in his condition. He didn't get better or worse. The only good news was the chest wound was healing. During the night, Shanice left Shawntale asleep and got up to use the bathroom. On the way back, she peeked into the room to check up on Pop. Queenie lay under the sheet next to him, talking.

"Did he wake up?" Shanice asked, stepping in the room.

"Nah. I'm just talkin', trynna let him know I'm here. I seen a movie where this bitch was in a coma, but she could hear everything happenin' around her. I'm keepin' him company just in case he can hear me."

"Well, I might as well come and do what I can to help," Shanice said, walking over and sitting on the bed. "Where is Princess?"

"Apparently her and Sasha became good friends while I was with you. They out."

"Good for her. I'm tired of her mugs. So, what you talkin' to Pop about?"

"About how he changed my life. I love the shit outta this nigga."

Hearing the tenderness in Queenie's voice made Shanice uncomfortable. Queenie noticed.

"C'mon, Shanice. You know how I feel about you and Pop."

Alarm spread across the pregnant woman's face as she looked at her cousin. "If he can hear us, don't you think you should watch what you say?"

"I don't like hidin' nothin' from Pop, so I told him."

Shanice panicked. "Oh my God! Why would you do that?"

"Because he my nigga. And I'm not sure if he can hear us. And because I wanted him to know so you can live with us."

Shanice shook her head. "I thought we was gon' tell him when the time is right? What are you talkin' 'bout?"

Queenie sat up, adjusting the sheet across her naked breasts as she moved closer to Shanice. "When Pop wakes up, I'm gon' tell him 'bout us. I don't want you to go back to Texas. I want you to be part of our family."

"What family? What the fuck you talkin' 'bout?"

"I want you to be a part of what we got. I haven't told you this because I wasn't sure how you would accept it, but me and my sister been fuckin' since we were kids. That's why it don't matter that Pop fuckin' her. The bond we all share is deep."

Shanice looked disgusted. "You fuck yo' sister? That's nasty. It's incest!"

"That's how you really feel? You think I'm nasty? I told you what the world considers normal may not be normal to us. We don't let nobody decide what we do. We do what makes us feel good. At church they told you lesbians was nasty, but you loved when I ate cho pussy, didn't you?"

"But that's different. I'm not yo' sister."

"So now you judging me? What about what happened at yo' house? I thought you was feelin' me."

Shanice looked away, her feelings and hormones confusing. "I don't know. You're giving me a lot. Too much. I don't know what to think."

Queenie grabbed Shanice's hands and held them. "Are you still feelin' me?"

It took her a while to answer. "Yes."

"Well then, kiss me."

"What about Pop?" Shanice frowned, looking at her cousin.

"If he can hear us, let him listen. We already said too much. Kiss me."

Shanice wouldn't move, so Queenie took charge, grabbing Shanice's face and kissing her aggressively. Queenie was naked beneath the sheet, and Shanice wore a t-shirt.

A Gangster's Code 2

"Oh, shit," Shanice moaned when Queenie slipped a finger into her pussy. When the shirt came off and Queenie began sucking the sensitive nipples, Shanice no longer cared she was about to have sex next to her comatose cousin. The fingers in her pussy and lips on her breasts had her high.

Then the feeling was gone. "Look!" Queenie said, pointing at Pop.

Shanice looked over and seen Pop had become aroused. His dick was making a tent in the sheet.

"He knows I'm here!" Shanice panicked, going for her shirt.

Queenie's eyes reflected excitement. "No! We might be able to wake him up. I tried suckin' his dick yesterday and it didn't get hard. Whatever is happenin' is because of you."

"What?" Shanice mugged, uncomfortable with the look on Queenie's face.

"It's you, Shanice. Pop is in love with you. That's why he won't fall in love with me."

"Gurl, you trippin'. Let me get outta here."

Queenie moved to stop her, climbing onto her lap. "Pop had a dream about you a couple months ago. He was fuckin' the mattress and sayin' yo' name. That's why he so protective of you. Think about it. Ain't no nigga ever been good enough for you. That's why he beat up C-Note. He was jealous. And now that we about to fuck, his dick get hard. He loves you, Shanice. In love. And he needs you to wake him."

Shanice wasn't convinced. "You sound crazy! Get the fuck off me! Let me up."

"No! Think about what I'm sayin'. I know it might sound crazy, but this is serious. Pop body is reactin' to you, not me."

Shanice looked disgusted. "And you think I'm s'posed to fuck my cousin?"

"Don't think about it like that. Just think about savin' his life," Queenie said, getting up and pulling the sheet off Pop Somethin'.

Shanice turned away, not wanting to see his naked body. "This shit is way too crazy."

Queenie walked over to stand in front of Shanice. "I'm his bitch. I know this sounds crazy, but I know what I'm talkin' 'bout. You have to save him. He loves you."

The women had a will-testing stare down before Shanice spoke. "I can't do it. I don't want to have sex with my cousin."

Queenie was desperate in wanting to bring Pop out of the coma. She didn't want to cry, but the tears didn't listen. "Please, Shanice. I know how this sounds. It's fucked up, I know. But this is where we at. And I swear to God, if we don't try everything we can to save him and he dies, I won't ever forgive you for this."

Shanice was stuck. Queenie's words were real, and the tears were unexpected. She felt a deep connection with the twin and could feel her pain, but fucking her cousin was unthinkable.

Unless it would save his life. "I can't believe I'ma agree to this, but okay."

Queenie's face expressed an unspeakable joy. "C'mon. Get on top. Hurry up."

Shanice closed her eyes and shook her head before going over to Pop. After straddling his lap, she closed her eyes again, grabbing his dick. The heart monitor beeped, scaring both women. "What the fuck was that?" Shanice asked, freezing in place.

"That's the heart monitor. He gettin' excited," Queenie explained. Then she moved forward and kissed Shanice, trying to put her at ease. "Go ahead. Put it in."

"I can't believe I'm doin' this," Shanice mumbled, closing her eyes and sitting on Pop's dick.

A Gangster's Code 2

The heart monitor beeped again, Pop's heart rate continuing to increase. Queenie bent over him, kissing him on the face and whispering in his ear. "Wake up, baby. Wake up. Me and Shanice here. Wake up and fuck us. Wake up."

Shanice was torn between pleasure and disgust as she rode her cousin's pipe. He was long and thick, and she would've loved it if it wasn't attached to family. When she looked down and seen Pop's eyes moving rapidly behind his eyelids, a tingle sparked through her body. Queenie was right. She was having an effect on Pop. It looked like he was trying to wake up.

"Fuck him harder! Do it faster," Queenie encouraged. She could see Pop trying to fight his way out of the coma. "Take the whole dick."

"Wait. It's big."

That wasn't good enough for Queenie. She straddled Pop's stomach, facing Shanice and pulled off the pregnant woman's t-shirt. "Fuck him like he me," she said, sucking Shanice's breasts and grabbing her hips to guide her.

The touch of her lesbian lover was what she needed to lose herself in the moment. She closed her eyes and allowed Queenie's hands to guide her hips. The taboo act of sex with a woman and her cousin sent sensations through her body that she couldn't describe. She increased the pace, riding Pop hard, loving the erotic deed.

"Yeah, baby. Fuck him good," Queenie cheered.

Pop's heart monitor beeped steadily, his excitement peaking. Then his body spasmed, locking up.

"What happened?" Queenie asked.

The sexiness of the moment was gone from Shanice's face. She looked disgusted. "He nutted in me. I feel so nasty."

"It's okay, baby. You did good," Queenie said, kissing her lips. "Is he still hard?"

Shanice climbed off, revealing his slick, rapidly-shrinking tool. Queenie moved quickly, slurping Pop into her mouth, trying to get him back hard. It was all for nothing. Pop's heart monitor beeped lightly as his heart rate slowed.

Chapter 15

Ever since the attack at Aunty Dorothy's house, Queenie had become a light sleeper. The slightest noise or bed movement would awaken her. So when the bed moved, Queenie's eyes opened immediately, finding the clutch that had been thrown onto the bed. Standing a few feet away was Princess, her face flat, eyes brimming with anger.

"Really, bitch? You gon' fuck her in the same bed as Pop?"

Queenie sat up and stretched out her arms, trying to calm her sister. "It ain't what you think. She almost made him wake up."

"I don't wanna hear that shit!" Princess snapped. "I told you not to fuck wit' her in the first place. You took it too far."

The raised voices woke Shanice. She lay in bed, listening to the sisters, unsure what to do.

"Just listen, Princess. Last night he woke up a little."

The beep of Pop's heart monitor made everyone pause. "What was that?" Princess asked.

"I think he 'bout to wake up!" Queenie said, moving to Pop and grabbing his face in both of her hands. "Can you hear me, baby? Wake up!"

The heart monitor beeped again, and Pop's eyes began moving rapidly behind his eyelids. And then they opened.

Queenie lost her mind. "*Oh my God! Oh my God! He woke up!*"

Princess and Shanice moved closer, watching Pop's eyes go from cloudy and confused to alert and coherent. Queenie removed the mask from his face. "Can you talk?"

He opened his mouth to speak, but no words came out. He tried again and only managed a whisper.

"What he say?" Princess asked eagerly.

"I don't know. Somebody get him somethin' to drink."

Shanice jumped out of bed and raced from the room. Pop cleared his throat, trying to speak again. Queenie moved her ear close to his lips and laughed.

"What he say?" Princess asked again.

"Why we makin' all this noise?" Queenie laughed, kissing him on the lips.

Princess didn't laugh. "I'ma leave that answer up to you."

Pop began whispering again. "You don't remember nothin'?" Queenie asked. He shook his head.

"What he say?" Princess asked.

"He wanna know what happened. Tell 'im."

"After you got shot, you called me and drove home. As soon as you parked, you passed out. Born Ready got you a doctor. You got a blood clot during the surgery and went in a coma. You been out for five days."

Pop frowned and whispered, "Five days?"

The sisters nodded. At that same moment, Shanice walked into the room with a bottle of water. A scowl spread over Pop's face as he mugged her. He tried to speak, but his words sounded like a hoarse dog trying to bark. Not being able to talk made him angry, and he ripped the IV from his arm. He sat up in bed and began barking again, none of them able to understand what he was saying. When Shanice held out the bottle of water, Pop snatched it, mugging her as he drank.

"What I tell you?" Princess scolded Queenie.

"How the fuck she get in my house?" Pop said, his voice harsh and deep.

"She came wit' me. When we heard you might die, she wanted to come check on you," Queenie explained.

The heart monitor beeped as Pop's anger rose. "What the fuck I tell you, Queenie? Fuck didn't you understand about that?"

A Gangster's Code 2

Queenie moved across the bed, creating distance between her and Pop. This was her first time on the receiving end of his anger, and she wasn't sure how he would react.

"Calm down, Pop," Princess interrupted.

He turned his anger on her. "Don't tell me to calm down, nigga! Y'all my bitches. When I say somethin', you mutha-fuckas don't go around and do what the fuck y'all wanna do. That ain't how this work. My word is law. My bitches don't break my law."

"Relax, cousin," Shanice cut in. "Your heart monitor is going crazy. You just woke up from a coma. Chill before you hurt yourself."

Pop looked at her like she was dog shit on the bottom of a fresh pair of Jordans. "Why the fuck is you still here?"

Shanice shrank back a little. Pop had never looked at her or spoken to her the way he did. "Because you never called me back. And you almost died. I came to see if you were okay."

"I'm good. Now get out."

Queenie came close, reaching out to Pop. "C'mon, baby. She the one that helped wake you up. Don't–"

A hard backhand to the face cut off Queenie's words, and she fell onto the bed.

"Shut the fuck up!" Pop roared. "I don't wanna hear that shit!" he breathed, physically tired from the slap.

Princess went for her clutch. The 380 leapt into her hand like it could walk. "Touch my sister again and she gon' be the last bitch you hit!"

Pop mugged Princess, breathing heavily, "You gon' shoot me, Princess? You gon' pull a gun on yo' nigga?"

Princess stood her ground. "Don't you ever touch her again, Pop, or I swear to God I'ma shoot yo' ass."

Pop eyed Princess, his limbs shaking as he struggled to get out of bed. "When I. Get up. I'm. Fuckin'. You up. You betta. Shoot me," he said weakly, struggling to breathe as he rose. The sheet slipped off, revealing his nakedness, his knees shaking like they were about to break.

Princess didn't back down, her finger holding steady on the trigger.

"Pop, Stop!" Queenie yelled, not wanting to see the outcome. She knew if Pop pushed his luck, Princess would kill him, but Pop didn't seem to care as he inched toward her. The closer he got, the more his body shook. When he could no longer take the physical strain, he collapsed and passed out.

***

When Pop opened his eyes, the first thing he noticed was Queenie. She sat in the middle of the bed, legs crossed Indian-style, watching him. A bruise had formed on the left side of her face, and her top lip showed swelling.

"That shit creepy as fuck," he mumbled.

She didn't speak right away. "Look what you did to my face."

"You shouldn'ta disobeyed me. I told you not to talk to Shanice. You know I don't bullshit. When I say somethin', I mean it. You my bitch. You went foul, and I had to put you back in yo' place."

The words hurt more than the slap. "You gon' talk to me like that, for real? I was worried about you. I love you. I brought her home and she helped you get better. We brought you back, nigga."

Pop's face twisted into a frown. "Fuck you talkin' 'bout?"

Queenie searched his face for a sign. Did he really not remember? "You don't know what happened last night?"

"I was in a coma. Fuck I s'posed to know what happened?"

Shanice walked in the room, the angry look on Pop's face halting the conversation. Then he seen the delicious-

A Gangster's Code 2

smelling bowl of chicken broth she carried on a plate. His mouth watered and stomach rumbled. He would've preferred fried chicken instead of broth, and something like some scalloped potatoes, but he correctly surmised that having just come out of a coma, his stomach wasn't quite up to that.

When he attacked the broth with fervor, she smiled with satisfaction. "Even though you shitted on me, I still got love for you."

Pop just kept on eating until the bowl was empty.

"What happened to C-Note?" Shanice asked, taking the plate.

Pop ignored her and got Queenie's attention. "Help me walk to the shower."

"You don't hear me talkin' to you, Paul?"

Pop didn't even acknowledge her presence. Instead, he wrapped the sheet around his waist and lifted a hand for Queenie to help him stand. Shanice pushed his arm down. "You ain't goin' nowhere 'til you talk to me! What happened to C-Note?"

Pop exploded, "I killed that bitch-ass nigga! He snitched. I don't fuck wit' snitches."

Silence echoed in the room. It took a couple seconds for the words to register in Shanice's brain. The reaction that followed was unbridled anger. Shanice ran at Pop, her nails turning into sharp claws as she reached for his face. Queenie leapt in the air, tackling Shanice onto the bed.

"Stop, Shanice!"

"Let me go! Let me go!" Shanice struggled.

"No. I can't. Stop."

The wrestling match was short-lived. Queenie was bigger and stronger. Shanice was pissed. Tears rolled down her face, and she stared up at Pop with angry eyes. "I hate you, Paul. I swear to God, I hate yo' guts. I don't ever wanna talk to you or see you again. Don't call me. Don't ask about me.

153

And if I die, don't come to my funeral, 'cause I damn sure ain't comin' to yours. Fuck you!"

***

"Welcome back to the land of the living!" Born Ready smiled, opening his arms for an embrace. "How you feel?"

Pop hugged him lightly, careful not to aggravate the chest wound. They were in Pop's living room. He was two days removed from the coma. Although he was able to move around, his strength hadn't returned and his body felt weak.

"I'm good. Can't nothin' keep a real nigga down."

"That's what I'm talkin' 'bout, nigga!" Born Ready grinned. "I need you now more than ever. While you was out, a lot of shit happened. We need to put our heads together and get back out there."

Pop shook his head. "I think I'm done."

Born Ready's face showed displeasure. "What you mean? We just got started, brah. The whole state can be S.O.D."

"I think I'ma take my quarter ticket and move on. Buck Wild is a loose cannon. Fuckin' wit' him gon' be the downfall. I ain't goin' down wit' the ship."

Born Ready paused to consider Pop's words. "Li'l bro is a hothead, I know. Nigga can't think past violence, which is why I need you to help me finish what we started. You a rare nigga, Pop. Gimme six months and I'ma have a mil for you. If you wanna leave after that, I won't try to stop you."

It was Pop's turn to stop and think. The money was tempting. His goal was literally a few months away, but no amount of money was worth dying or spending life in a cell. "Did Buck tell you what happened?"

"Yeah. Said twelve was watchin' the house and you had it out wit' 'em while he ran in to get D.D. Said you ran and left him."

Pop laughed. "So that's how he spun it, huh?"

A Gangster's Code 2

"Yeah. I know he left some shit out. Gimme yo' version."

"I seen twelve in the truck as soon as we got to the house. I told the stupid-ass nigga to fall back, but he broke the patio door and ran in the house anyway. They ran up wit' they dogs out. We let 'em bark. They almost knocked me off. Hell yeah, I left his stupid ass."

"Listen, Pop. That's li'l brah, and I can't turn my back on him. But I had a feelin' you would say what you said. I try to anticipate er'thang. Look outside. That's you."

After a brief stare down, Pop got up with effort and looked out the window. In the driveway was a black-on-black Lamborghini Aventador.

"That's a couple years old. A $150,000 car. Bitch look like the Batmobile, don't it, Pop?" Born Ready asked, his words enticing Pop. "Stay wit' the team, brah. Help me finish what we started and that's you, plus the mil."

Pop wasn't materialistic. He liked nice things, but he wasn't the kind of person who lived to be seen. As far as he was concerned, reaching a mil was his only goal, but he couldn't take his eyes off the powerful, high-performance machine. It called his name.

"Fuck it. Where the keys at?"

***

It didn't take Pop long to learn how to drive the Lambo. The eight-speed automatic, 600 horsepower engine excited Pop every time he pressed the gas pedal. Sport seats molded to his body, the top-of-the-line leather interior smelled new, and the black aluminum wheels made the car a perfect ride. Fifteen minutes later, Pop and Born Ready pulled into the parking lot of Scandalous. It was one in the afternoon, so there weren't many patrons in the strip club. One of the few men in the club caught Pop's eye. Dark skin, over six feet tall, wirey build, short afro, trimmed mustache, dressed casually in a t-shirt, jeans, and Nikes. The 40-year-old cop gave all his attention to the thick, light-skinned, half-naked woman grinding on his lap.

"'Sup, detective!" Born Ready nodded. "I see you gettin' the party started early."

Darnell Marks looked away from the entertainment to eye his guests. His eyes lingering on Pop Somethin'. "No sense in lettin' good talent go to waste. You look familiar."

Pop Somethin' eyed the detective, staying silent.

"Can we join you?" Born Ready asked.

"Yeah. Y'all want drinks?"

Born Ready sat down heavily. "Yeah. A beer would be nice."

Pop shook his head, choosing to remain silent as he took a seat.

"Grab us some brews. Put it on my tab," Marks told the stripper, patting her on the ass as she scooted away. "Is your boy a mute?" he asked, looking Pop over again.

"Nah. He actually really articulate and eloquent with his speech, but you don't understand his language, so don't worry."

"I shot somebody the other day after he shot my partner. Had the same aura as your guy. Was it him?"

Born Ready got serious. "I don't know what you talkin' 'bout, and that's not why we here."

The detective laughed. "Okay. I'm a naturally curious person, so don't shoot me for trying. Now, tell me how you got my number and what you want."

"You a public servant, mane. Yo' information is public record. But I also heard you did jobs for the people you serve and protect, if the price is right. You see what's goin' on in the streets. I need a man on the inside. S.O.D. takin' a lot of losses. Tell me what I need to know to protect my people and assets."

A Gangster's Code 2

The detective sat back in the chair, holding eye contact with Born Ready. "I became a cop to heal my city. To put criminals in jail. To protect those that couldn't protect themselves. Along the way I seen crime on a whole 'nother level. When I was on the beat, I chased down petty drug dealers and robbers, convinced I was taking a bite out of crime. Turns out the people on the streets aren't criminals, but victims of the greedy judges, politicians, and dirty cops. I discovered that everyone is doing the same thing. Just trynna make it. Currency is power."

"That almighty dolla!" Born Ready smiled.

"I need ten thousand up front. Another five every time I drop you something golden."

Born Ready dug into his pocket and threw four bound stacks of money on the table. "That's twenty. A lot more where that came from. Now gimme somethin' gold wit' diamonds in it."

Detective Marks grabbed the money and fanned through it. "We believe S.O.D. is trying to take over the drug game in Atlanta. We think y'all killed Grind Squad's co-founder, Sid, and their enforcer, Duke. How do we know? We have a witness. She was on the phone when your boys made the hit. Said she heard the killer say, and I quote, "It's a takeover, bitch. S.O.D. in the building.""

"Who is she?"

"I don't have access to that information."

"I just gave you twenty Gs. Get it."

"I'll see what I can do. It's not my investigation. Blank is the lead man. Somethin' else you should know is we're focusing on different leads in the S.O.D. leaders' homicides. Nobody believes Mecca killed Boss and Gus and ran away with the money. We also don't believe Grind Squad made the hits. And now that we've had this meeting, I'm sure you are the brains behind the shake-up in Atlanta. Good job."

J-Blunt

"Yo' job is to keep yo' people off our ass by keepin' me two steps ahead. You do yo' job and I'ma keep them pockets right. You got my numba. Hit me."

Chapter 16

"Have you heard from Pop?" Queenie asked.

Princess didn't look up from washing the dishes. "Nope."

Queenie sat heavily in the kitchen chair. "It's been four days and he ain't called or answered the phone. I don't know what to do. Should I file a police report? I already checked all the jails and hospitals."

Princess threw the dishrag in the sink and spun to face her sister. "This is why I told yo' ass not to fall in love! No, don't call the police. You seen how Pop was actin' before he left. He didn't talk to us, fuck us, or sleep in the same bed. I pulled a gun on him. Yo' stupid-ass fucked Shanice and then convinced her to fuck Pop. If I was Pop, I wouldn't talk to our ass, neither."

"But he don't remember nothin'. He was in a coma."

"That's not the point, Queenie. He mad. He feel betrayed. I know how Pop think. He ain't goin' nowhere. He thinkin' it out his own way. He comin' back. He operates on principles, not emotions. Loyalty. He knows what he has in us. He knows we'll be there when he calls. It's a waiting game. He'll come back when he ready."

"I hope you right, 'cause I miss him."

"He will. Trust me. Have you talked to Shanice? How is she doin'?"

Sadness shown in Queenie's eyes. "Pop hurt her. I think she really hate him."

"You know you played a part in all this, right? You shouldn't have brought her in this. You tried to manipulate her and Pop, and it backfired. Hope you learned yo' lesson."

"I know. I fell bad about everything. I wish I could fix it. And you wanna hear somethin' crazy?"

Princess knew Queenie was about to drop a bomb. "What?"

"I like Shanice for real. I wanna keep her around."

Princess shook her head. "You just ain't gon' learn, is you?"

Beyoncé and Jay-Z's *Drunk in Love* played as Queenie's phone rang. Her eyes lit up and her heart skipped a beat as she raced to answer. "Hey, baby! Where you at? Why didn't you come home?"

Pop's voice was flat, devoid of any emotion. "Princess wit' chu?"

"Yeah. I got it on speaker. She can hear you."

"I'ma be outta town for a couple more days. I need y'all to take care of somethin' for me. Earn my trust back. Y'all betrayal cut me deep. I think y'all need anotha trial by fire. Get up wit' Born Ready, and he gon' let ch'all know the move. Don't try to call me. I ain't gon' answer."

"Wait, Pop! Where you at?" Queenie called.

"Bitch, he hung up. You heard what he said. Call Born Ready. Let's do what we gotta do to bring this nigga back home."

***

Pop lay the phone down and closed his eyes, thinking about his twin bitches. They had become parts of him, like an extra set of hands. Or eyes. He trusted them completely, knowing their loyalty was true, but they had betrayed him. Princess pulling the gun was understandable. She was protecting her little sister like she had their whole life. But Queenie's actions were unexpected. Her love for him was making her slip, and that had to be punished. She went against him, and not only did she get in contact with Shanice, but fucked her.

Pop let out a long breath when his cousin entered his mind. The pain on her face and in her voice haunted him, threatening to undo his sanity. He never wanted to hurt her or cause her pain, but he did. She tried to attack him. But it was her fault. He warned her about getting involved with street niggas.

He reached for the blunt in the ashtray, lighting it and taking a long pull. Regret washed over him as he breathed out a cloud of smoke. He wished he hadn't handled her so rough, but her love for C-Note clouded his judgment. The truth burned in his chest as he took another puff of loud. He was jealous of C-Note. Queenie was right. He loved Shanice, had been in love with her since they were kids. But incest was unthinkable until she brought him out of the coma. He'd dreamed about fucking her every night since he'd woken. She had become a need, which is why he hurt her feelings. He purposely drove a wedge between them, forever keeping them apart. To protect his sanity, he needed to stay as far away from Shanice as possible. It was the only way.

Movement in the bed make him look over. The nurse was waking from sleep. The Columbian was a dime, soft tan skin, pretty eyes, juicy lips, and a perfect smile. She reached out to Pop, running a hand through his beard.

"Good morning, *papi.*"

"'Sup?"

"I wish I could wake up next to you every morning," she purred, rubbing his face and neck, stopping at the healed scar on his chest.

"My life is too complicated right now. Plus, not bein' around you make, it special when we do get together."

After rubbing the scar, the nurse's hands moved farther down his body, grabbing his meat. "Oh. You wake up ready, don't you?"

"Gotta stay ready so you won't have to get ready."

"Good one," she laughed, stroking him. "I want to thank you again for what you did for me. My life feels like mine again. I don't know how you got him to shoot himself, but–"

Pop cut her off. "I don't know what you talkin' 'bout."

She gave him a long stare. Pop's gaze reflected his position on pillow talk about business. "I'm sorry. I should've known better. But I'm free now. And if you ever need me, don't hesitate to call. I will take care of whatever you need."

Pop looked down at her hand rubbing his dick. "If you take care of that, I would be forever indebted."

She moved closer and kissed the bullet scar on his chest. "Your wish is my command."

***

Detective Blank felt like a lucky man. In the 49 years he'd walked the planet, he never got the chance to witness anything like he hoped he was about to see when he closed the hotel door. He was short and chubby, balding on the crown of his head, and looked like a Danny DeVito impersonator, but the women on his right and left arm made him feel like he was the handsomest man in the world. Queenie pressed her body into the smaller man as they walked toward the cheap room. Her dreads were piled atop her head in a wrap, and she wore a tight, black mini-dress and heels. The curves of her body and bouncing backside had the white man's dick dripping precum. On his right arm was Princess, dressed similarly to Queenie, his hand gripping the soft flesh of her ass like it was a grocery bag.

As soon as they walked in the hotel room, Blank told them what he wanted. "You two on the bed. I wanna watch first. This is so fuckin' hot, and my dick's been dripping since I seen you kiss at the bar."

When the cop took a seat in the chair, the sisters knelt in the center of the bed, kissing each other passionately and grabbing ass. The dresses came off a few seconds later, and the sisters took turns sucking each other's breasts. When Queenie lay back, Princess dove between her legs face-first.

The heavy action had the cop more turned on than he had ever been in his life. Instead of undressing, he pulled his dick

162

A Gangster's Code 2

through the zipper and began jacking off. Watching the dark-skinned sisters committing the taboo act had him busting a nut in a couple minutes.

Princess looked up when he moaned. The detective had nutted all over his hand and pants. "Come over here and let us get that back hard for you."

A lustful grin spread across his face as the cop stripped down to his boxers.

"Get them cuffs," Queenie said.

After grabbing the cuffs, he crawled onto the bed and gave them to Princess. "Cuff me up good," he grinned.

Princess cuffed him to the headboard. As soon as they were sure he was helpless, the sexual atmosphere changed to serious. Queenie went for her purse, pulling out a pair of switchblades.

"Hey! No sharp objects," the detective protested.

"No, baby. We need these to get what we want," Queenie smiled, crawling toward him with the six-inch blade.

Blank got mad and began yelling. "You stupid bitches! Uncuff me right now! I'm done playin' games. Somebody help!"

Princess stuffed his own socks in his mouth to muffle the screams. "Shut the fuck up! You sound like a li'l bitch. Tell us what we want so we can get the fuck outta her. Who told you S.O.D. killed Sid and Duke?"

He mumbled something. Princess removed the socks.

"I ain't tellin' you bitches nothin'! Help! Somebody help!"

Princess stuffed the sock back in his mouth as Queenie's knife dug into his belly. Instead of pulling it out, she twisted, trying to get it deeper. Blank's muffled screams filled the room, and he bucked away from the blade. Queenie snatched the knife out and watched blood gush from the wound.

"Damn, gurl!" Princess said, a little disgusted.

"His punk-ass trynna be tough! Tell us the bitch name, white boy. Who is she?" Queenie said, putting the knife to his throat.

When he began mumbling again, Princess pulled the sock from his mouth. Instead of telling them what they wanted to know, he spit in Princess's face and began thrashing around wildly. "Help! Help! I'm a police officer! Help!"

Princess tried to stuff the sock back in his mouth, but he shook his head, continuing to thrash around wildly. Queenie jumped from the bed and grabbed his service gun. "Quit screamin' 'fore I shoot yo' bitch-ass!"

He calmed at the sight of his Glock 9. "Please, ladies, don't do this. You don't know what you're doing. If you kill me, the whole S.O.D. organization will go down."

Princess straddled his lap to keep him from bucking around, then she put the knife to his dick, applying just enough pressure to make him whine. "Gimme the bitch name or I'ma re-circumcise yo' ass."

"Listen to what I'm telling you. You will not get away with killing me. *Ah!*"

Princess dug the knife deep into his dick and balls. He screamed so loud Queenie ran over to cover his face with a pillow. When Princess snatched the knife out, Queenie waited for him to calm down before removing the pillow. The detective was in the worst pain. He wouldn't stop sweating, his face and body red from pain and anger.

"Okay," he moaned. "Her name is Melissa Robinson. She lives over by Pittsburgh. But don't think this is over for you bitches. I'm going–"

Queenie smashed the pillow on his face and began stabbing him in the chest. Princess joined, stabbing him in the stomach repeatedly. The detective's body jerked and spasmed as the sisters stabbed over a hundred times apiece. They didn't stop stabbing until he stopped moving. When they came from the blood trance, blood was everywhere, all over the bed, the twins, and the walls. Princess looked at her

A Gangster's Code 2

hands in amazement. They were covered in the cop's life fluids.

"Oh shit!"

Queenie didn't seem phased at all. "C'mon. Let's clean up so we can get the fuck outta here."

Princess walked like she was in a trance as she followed Queenie to the shower. "You okay?" Queenie asked, noticing the dazed and disoriented look on her sister's face.

"I-I don't know. That shit was crazy."

Queenie grabbed the bar of soap and towel, joining Princess in the shower. "That shit was a rush. I felt his life drainin'. I feel like a goddess. My pussy wet as fuck!"

Princess continued to look dazed, then she reached down and rubbed her pussy, surprised to find it wet. "Damn. I'm wet, too. I feel weird. And horny."

Queenie stopped washing and pulled Princess close. After tonguing her, she kissed her way down Princess's bloody body, getting on her knees and sucking her pussy. When she came, Princess returned the favor. When they finished showering, the sisters cleaned the room as well as they could before setting it on fire.

***

Me-Me loved the attention she got when she put on clothes that flaunted her curvy body. The Dominican and black beauty stood 5'3" and weighed 140 pounds. Her 36Cs jiggled in the low-cut blouse, so much cleavage on display her areolas showed. The white yoga pants flexed her phat ass, thick thighs, and fat pussy lips. The long, fake ponytail bounced with the sway of her hips every time her red bottoms clicked the concrete. Men, women, and children stopped what they were doing to take a look as the bronze-skinned angel passed by.

J-Blunt

When the dark-colored Crown Victoria slowed and began keeping pace with her, Me-Me knew what to expect. When the tinted window rolled down, a man would ask her where she was going and if she needed a ride. If he was handsome or looked like he had money, she would get in. If he was ugly or broke, she would keep on moving.

As soon as she finished her thought, the passenger window rolled down. Instead of a man, Me-Me was surprised by the sight of beautiful, dark-skinned twin sisters. The passenger smiled flirtingly. "Excuse me. Are you Me-Me?"

The temptress immediately assessed the situation. She didn't know the women but they showed no hostility. They were polite and smiled. Nothing seemed out of the ordinary. "Yeah. I'm Me-Me. Do I know you?"

"Melissa Robinson?" Queenie asked, making sure.

A red light went off in Me-Me's mind. How did she know her real name? Was it drama? Did she fuck her man?

When Queenie noticed the nervous look on the woman's face, she laughed and smiled. "Relax, girl. We not on bullshit. I got somethin' for you, and I just wanna make sure you who we lookin' for. I don't want to give this to the wrong person."

Hearing she was about to receive something changed Me-Me's demeanor, and the smile was back. "Yeah, I'm Melissa. What you got for me? Who is it from?"

"Duke want you to meet him, bitch!"

Me-Me didn't have time to figure out the riddle. Queenie pointed the Glock 9 she had taken from Detective Blank and filled Me-Me's body with bullets.

Chapter 17

Pop Somethin' loved the Batmobile more than any material possession he'd ever owned. The Lambo was perfect. Fast, sleek, and powerful. If he could transform into a car, it would be the Lambo. As he drove down Peach Tree, he loved the looks he got from admirers and haters. Things had been going well since he'd come back to Atlanta. Detective Marks fed S.O.D. information steadily, keeping them two steps ahead of the police, and the war with Grind Squad looked to be over since the crew had gone into hiding. For now, the streets belonged solely to S.O.D. Pop's mil looked close.

At Ponce de Leon Avenue was a strip club called Kitty's. After parking the Batmobile, Pop went inside. It didn't take him long to find who he was looking for. Well, actually, she found him.

"Hey, baby!" Queenie smiled, jumping off the barstool and running into Pop's arms.

"Damn, gurl. You actin' like I didn't just see you this mornin'."

"Can't a bitch be happy to see her nigga? Even if you leave for five minutes, I miss you. That's how you know the love real."

Pop chuckled. "Okay. If you say so. Where Princess? Y'all ready to go?"

"She should be out in a minute. She was bleedin' these niggas, baby. She just got in the shower. Oh, and Buck Wild here."

Pop acted like she didn't mention the name. "How y'all like it here?"

"It's okay. It ain't nothin' like we was doin' in Dallas, but it's okay. Keeps us outta yo' way and gives us somethin' to do. We ain't complainin'."

"I never asked you this before, but what's the plan when y'all can't strip no more?"

"I don't know. This all we really know. My goal is to get to Jamaica with you, help you with the hotel. That's the plan, right?"

"Yeah. Nothin' changed. I just wanted to know if y'all had a backup plan."

"We all in wit' chu, baby. Nothin' else matters."

"Pop! C'mere!"

He looked toward the dressing room and seen Princess waving, a panicked look on her face.

"What up?"

"Buck Wild in the VIP going crazy. He drunk. Somebody need to calm him down before–"

A loud crash and raised voices came from the short hallway behind the bar. Pop walked over and seen a security guard laid out on the floor. "Stupid-ass fuck-nigga!" Pop mumbled, walking toward the commotion. The VIP room's door was split in half. Inside the room Buck Wild was in a wrestling match with two guards. A stripper was pressed against the wall, watching the melee with wide eyes.

"Buck! What the fuck you doin'?" Pop called.

The big man's head spun slowly toward Pop, a drunken smile on his face. "Help me, dawg! These pussy-niggas think they can fuck in mine. Get one and I'ma whoop this otha nigga!"

Pop stepped into the room and in the middle of the brawl. "Aye, let him go, y'all! Let him go! I got him. I'ma get him outta here."

After a little more struggle, the security guards backed away and went to their fallen comrade.

"I had they ass, Pop! Niggas can't fuck in mine!" Buck Wild bragged.

"A'ight, brah. Let's get the fuck outta here. You parked outside, right?"

A Gangster's Code 2

"Wait, wait, Pop. Hold up. I gotta get my dick sucked first. I gave that bitch fifty for some top. I want my dick sucked."

"I'm not touchin' that nigga dick," the stripper cut in, still pressed against the wall. She looked terrified, like she had seen a monster.

"Nah! Fuck dat! I paid for some head. I want my dick sucked!" Buck Wild yelled angrily, making a move toward the frightened dancer.

Pop grabbed his arm. "Chill, nigga. Let's go 'fore they call twelve. That shit light. Just find anotha bitch."

"I tried to give him the money back," the woman said. "It's on the floor."

Pop looked down and seen the green bill near the table. "Keep it." Then he turned to Buck. "I'ma find you a bad bitch. C'mon so we won't have to bag nobody."

After a little more effort, Pop was able to coax the drunken goon outside. He was in no condition to drive, so Pop led him to the Batmobile and gave Queenie the keys to Buck Wild's Benz.

"When you gon' let me fuck Queenie in her fat ass?" Buck slurred.

"Never. You can't handle my bitches, nigga."

"Psh! I'll handle them hos better than you can!"

Pop laughed. "You can't do nothin' betta than me except act a fool, nigga."

Buck Wild took the dig personal, pushing Pop Somethin' away "Fuck you think you talkin' too, nigga? Born Ready ain't here to save yo' ass now. What up, nigga?"

Pop Somethin wanted to tear off into Buck, but he knew the drunken man didn't stand a chance. "Just get in the car before I leave you, nigga."

Buck Wild turned up, getting belligerent. "Fuck dat! Fight me like a man, pussy-nigga! It's me and you, Pop. Right here."

Pop stared at him like he was a stupid fool, then Buck Wild took a swing, almost losing balance as he whiffed on the punch. Pop tried to keep his anger in check. "Don't make me beat cho ass out here. Get in the car, nigga!"

Buck Wild took another wild swing, missing by a mile, his momentum making him stumble. Pop was sober, bigger, and faster. He stepped toward Buck, throwing a hard right uppercut. The blow landed perfectly on Buck Wild's chin, lifting him off the ground. The inebriated thug was knocked out in midair. He landed on his back a few feet away, his head smacking the ground with a sickening thud. Pop didn't intend to hurt him, just knock him out so he could get him home, but when he heard the way his head hit the ground, he knew Buck might not get back up. So he stood over him and slapped him across the face.

"Buck! Buck! Get up, nigga!"

The unhinged man didn't move, stir, or flinch, and that's when Pop noticed the pool of blood forming on the concrete behind his head.

"Fuck! Stupid-ass nigga!" Pop cursed, looking around to see if anyone witnessed the accidental murder. The coast looked clear, so Pop dragged the lifeless body toward the Lambo.

Headlights shining on the Batmobile made Pop look up in alarm. It was Buck's Benz. "What the fuck happened?" Princess asked, climbing from the passenger seat.

"Open that back door. Stupid-ass nigga tried me, so I knocked his ass out. He hit his head. Stupid-ass nigga dead."

Princess opened the back door of the Benz and helped Pop put the body in the back seat. "What we gon' do wit' the body?"

"Make his ass disappear. Y'all follow me."

***

A Gangster's Code 2

The stress lines on Born Ready's face aged him ten years in just two days. Bags beneath his eyes and stubble atop his normally clean-shaven head spoke more of his state of mind than he expressed with words. When he sat in the passenger seat of the Batmobile, he looked more like a man who's world was falling apart than the leader of a million-dollar drug organization.

"Still no word?" Pop asked.

Born Ready let out a long breath. "Nah. Damn, Pop. I know somebody clipped my nigga. I feel it."

"Buck Wild is an animal, brah. Maybe he just gettin' carried away wit' that porno bitch. I can't see nobody gettin' him out the way that easy."

Pain reflected in Born Ready's eyes when he looked at Pop Somethin'. "I know what you trynna do, brah, but we both know what it is. We been in the gutta too long to pretend it's a silver linin' in the clouds. I know he gone. I just wanna find his body and send him home so our old lady can say bye. And whenever I find out who killed my nigga, I'm killin' everybody that nigga ever loved."

Pop didn't have any words to say, so he kept quiet. The hurting man wasn't to be played with or taken lightly. Born Ready was a capable adversary, and Pop seen him as an equal. Even though he was sure Buck Wild's death wouldn't come back to him, he planned to keep his eyes open.

After a short and silent drive, Pop parked the Batmobile outside Scandalous. They walked in and spotted Detective Marks being entertained by the same woman from the previous meeting. When the cop seen Born Ready and Pop Somethin', he shooed the woman away.

"What up, Marks?" Born Ready asked as he and Pop had seats.

The detective wore a serious look. "Killing a cop wasn't part of the plan!"

Born Ready played the part. "What the fuck you talkin' 'bout?"

"You killed Blank. Or had him killed. And the witness. If this gets back to me, I'm fucked. They're digging up all the dirt on every cop in the city to get a lead. They know somebody put the word out. You went too far."

"Relax, mane. Don't get to wiggin' out on me. Whatever happened to Blank and that witness ain't on you, and it ain't no way it can get back to you. This the big leagues, homeboy. Big fish don't swim in ponds. I'm payin' you to be my man on the inside and that's what I need you to do."

"But I didn't know a cop would get killed and all our asses would get examined."

"Work hazard," Born Ready said easily.

"Easy for you to say. You don't have co-workers trying to put you in jail for the rest of your life."

"You right. My peers trynna kill me, so chill. You bein' paranoid. They not investigatin' you, but if you keep panicking, then yo' ass gon' end up way up north wit' niggas that don't care if they stick they dicks in a nigga ass or a bitch pussy. Chill, mane. Er'thang gon' be a'ight."

The detective rubbed his face and lit a cigarette. "Yeah. Okay. I'll try to do that. Easier said than done."

Born Ready pulled out a stack of bills and threw it on the table. "My brotha ain't been home in two days. His name is Reese Cummings. Look into it and get back to me. He drove a silver 750 Benz, license plate SCT750. When you know somethin', let me know."

***

Detective Marks had the feeling he was being followed. He had been feeling that way for a couple of days. He wasn't sure if it was a co-worker, the feds, or someone off the street, and every time he tried to find the tail, he couldn't. So he continued with his investigation of Reese Cummings, AKA Buck Wild.

When he learned Reese had escaped from prison, the investigation became exciting. He used traffic cameras to locate the car on the day of the disappearance. It was last seen being driven by two women at a stop light on Ponce de Leon, being trailed by a black Lamborghini. More traffic cameras revealed the driver of the black sports car to be the same man that had attended the meets with Born Ready. The same man he believed shot his partner outside D.D.'s house.

As he sat at the desk trying to connect the dots, he realized S.O.D. was imploding. Again. It started with the takeover by Born Ready and the murders of Boss, Gus, and Mecca. Now the murder of Buck Wild threatened to send the clique into an internal war. S.O.D. wouldn't be around much longer. He needed to find out what happened to Reese as soon as possible. The information was extremely valuable in the right hands. Early retirement flashed in his mind as he got up from the desk and headed for his car.

Kitty's wasn't far from the station. After speaking with the owner, he was given a list of the 25 women who worked at the club. There were 15 women working the night Reese disappeared. Two of them were seen in the 750 Benz.

After making some calls, he learned the women used fake names and didn't list a home address on their job applications. Red flags went off in his head. Who were the women, and why didn't they want to be found? The only way to get answers was to interview their co-workers. After nine interviews, he found the information that would make him a rich man.

"Hell yeah, I remember his nasty ass! I'll never forget what he put me through," Valery Simpson said, still shaken by the encounter with the man shown on the detective's phone.

J-Blunt

"Can you tell me what happened the night you seen him? I believe he committed a very serious crime, and I'm trying to piece together his steps. Anything you can remember will help out. I want him in a cell for the rest of his life."

Valery looked eager to help. "He came in here about a week ago. I thought he was cute, and I heard him say he was S.O.D., so I knew he had money. After I danced for him, we went to V.I.P. When we were alone, he got aggressive and paid me for extras. Then he pulled out the biggest, ugliest dick I ever seen in my life. Scared the shit out of me, and I tried to leave. He got rough, so I screamed and security came in. They started fighting, but he was fucking them up. And then another man, who was bigger than all of them, came in."

The detective cut her off. "Describe the new guy."

"He was tall and built. Had dreadlocks and a big beard."

"Had you ever seen him before?"

She nodded. "Yeah. He came to pick up the new girls a couple times. The twins. Queenie and Princess."

"Do you know the next time Queenie and Princess will be at work?"

"Nah. They new, so they don't get the good hours. You have to talk to Brian about that."

"Okay. Finish telling me about your encounter with the man in the picture. You were saying the guy with the dreadlocks came in the room."

"He was cool. He came in and calmed the other man down. I think his name was Buck Wild. Then they left."

"Okay. If you remember anything else, I want you to call me. You've been a great help. Take my card and call me."

The smile on Detective Mark's face grew wider with every step he took toward the unmarked car. He had the who, the when, and the where. All he needed was the why and how. Those two questions were worth a lot of zeroes. As he climbed in the car, he noticed the full moon in the cloudless sky. It was late, and he was tired. After a stop at the station,

174

he would clock out and go home, but not before he made a call. He wanted to drop a teaser. Not too much, but just enough to open the safe.

"What chu got?" Born Ready answered.

"We need to meet."

"Why? What you got? You found my brother?"

"No. But I think I know what happened to him. And so does someone close to you."

"Fuck that mean? Who?"

The detective heard the eagerness in Born Ready's voice. It was exactly what he wanted. Now it was time for the cliff-hanger. "I can't talk about it right now. I'm on assignment. But we'll meet tomorrow. Make sure you bring a fatter envelope. It's worth it. Trust me."

The ride back to the station was filled with pleasant thoughts on how he would invest the money he'd been collecting. So far he'd gotten over fifty thousand dollars from S.O.D. Another fifty would put him over the top.

One hundred thousand dollars of tax-free money consumed his thoughts as he parked behind the station. Contentment and a false sense of security stopped the detective from paying much attention to his surroundings. After getting out of the car and checking to make sure the door was locked, the feeling he was being watched made the detective's skin itch. He looked over his shoulder and spotted the big, black figure advancing. An alarm rang in his mind as he went for the service pistol.

He never got the chance to release it from the holster. Ten bullets from the assailant's gun tore into the detective's face, neck and chest.

J-Blunt

Chapter 18

Pop lay in bed, staring up at the ceiling, lost in thought. A few months ago the move to Atlanta seem like a great idea. He had to leave Texas, and the promise of riches and a good time was a dream come true, but now that he made money and put in work, the decision to stay with Born Ready and complete phase three didn't' seem like such a good idea. The bodies were piling up, and two police among the deceased had the city on fire. S.O.D., Grind Squad, and everybody connected to them were being harassed by the police. It was only a matter of time before they got on Pop's trail. He couldn't allow that to happen. It was time to make an exit.

"Mm!" Princess moaned, pulling Pop from his thoughts. "Move, bitch! It's my turn."

"Nah. I got it. I suck dick better than you, anyway. Don't I, baby?" Queenie asked, wrestling Pop's dick from Princess.

"Aye, y'all betta chill 'fore I don't let nobody suck it. Play nice," he admonished playfully.

"And if we don't?" Princess asked, taking the tip of his dick in her mouth and biting lightly.

A jolt of pain shot though Pop's body, and he sucked in a sharp breath. "You betta chill before I take over. And I ain't gon' be nice."

Princess took more of him into her mouth, looking him in the eyes as she bit down. Pain and pleasure shot through his body, making him wince. And then he reacted. He had fully healed from the chest wound, his strength and speed back. After snatching his dick from her mouth, he manhandled Princess, flipping her onto her back, throwing a leg onto his shoulder, and entering her roughly.

"Oh shit, baby!" Princess moaned, putting a hand on his stomach to slow him from going too deep.

"Get her, baby!" Queenie cheered.

J-Blunt

"You think I won't fuck you up?" Pop growled, snatching her hand away and digging deep into her pussy until their pelvises were touching.

Princess loved the roughness. "Fuck you, nigga. I ain't nice, either."

Pop lifted a hand to her throat, choking her as he fucked her with long, deep strokes. When he hit his zone, Pop threw her other leg on his shoulder, fucking her fast and hard. Princess tried to get away, but Queenie helped him keep her in place.

"Nah, bitch! Take that dick! You was talkin' that shit," Queenie laughed.

When the orgasm racked through Princess's body, Pop let go of her legs and backed away, holding his dick like it was a weapon. "Yeah. Talk that shit now."

Princess stared up at him, trying to catch her breath, unable to speak.

"Like I thought," Pop laughed.

"C'mon, baby. Let me show her how thick bitches take that dick," Queenie said, getting on her knees, face down, ass up.

Pop moved the weapon toward Queenie and gave her what she wanted. Her ass bounced and jiggled as he slammed his pelvis into it.

"Oh, shit, baby! Yeah, daddy!" she moaned, throwing it back at him.

Pop slapped her ass and continued giving her long, deep strokes. When he felt Princess's hand on his nuts, a shock of electricity passed through his body. She continued massaging and squeezing his balls while he fucked her sister. Pop didn't want to bust, but Princess's hand and Queenie's pussy was too much for one man.

"Awe, shit!" he grunted, shooting off in Queenie before falling back onto the bed.

Queenie spun around, grabbing hold of his dick and sucking her and her sister's juices from it. "My pussy taste better, don't it, baby?" Queenie asked between slurps.

Princess shoved the side of her sister's head as she lay next to Pop. "Hell nah! You need to learn how to suck dick better. You know I be slayin' that dragon. Don't I, Pop?"

"C'mon, y'all. We ain't finna go there. Y'all both my bitches, and I like the way both y'all do it. No favorites."

"That was so weak," Princess laughed.

"But it's true. I can't pick. That's why I need both of y'all. It's like peanut butter and jelly. Can't have one without the other."

"I'm jelly," Queenie said, slapping her ass and making it jiggle.

After sharing a laugh, Princess got serious. "What you think about everything that's happening, Pop? I think we might be burnin' up the ATL."

"I was just thinkin' 'bout that. This bitch on fire. S.O.D. ain't gon' make it. I think we should pull out before shit hit the fan."

Queenie stopped sucking Pop to join in. "How much money we got?"

"'Bout $400,000. Right where we was before they burned down the house."

"Do you think we can get the mil? $400,000 is a lot, but it ain't the goal."

"I don't know. I'm thinkin' we should leave wit' somethin' while we got the opportunity. Born Ready is a smart nigga, but he blinded by greed. Plus, killin' Marks gon' get back to S.O.D. sooner than niggas think. That's gon' be on Born Ready. Feds 'bout to get involved once they connect the dots. They prolly find out about Buck Wild and the stripper since Marks was able to do it. That li'l stripper bitch can tell them 'bout us." Pop paused to let out a breath. "This shit 'bout to get real messy. Plus, I don't think we heard the last of Grind Squad. I got a feelin' er'thang finna pop off. Question is, when?"

"All I want is for us to stay together," Queenie said. "We almost lost you, and I don't wanna go through that again."

Pop looked down and seen the tears filling her eyes. "Quit, girl. I'm immortal. Can't nobody kill me but God."

"I say we get the fuck outta here," Princess cut in. "I agree with you, baby. Ain't no tellin' when this shit gon' blow. We put in too much work to leave empty-handed."

***

Thinking about what could've happened to Buck Wild made Born Ready feel like he was drowning in boiling water. How did he die? Who killed him? Marks said somebody close knew what happened. The closest people were Sasha, B-Real, and Pop Somethin'. Sasha wasn't a killer. B-Real was capable of killing, capable of betrayal, and most certainly not to be trusted. And then there was Pop Somethin'. Certified goon. Killed without hesitation. A physical beast. He played the streets how LeBron played basketball. Unstoppable. One of the three had knowledge about Buck's disappearance, and when he found out who it was, Born Ready was going to make sure that person and everybody involved with them would die bloody deaths.

"I never understood why you did that," Sasha said, flopping down on the couch next to Born Ready. She was wearing her classic outfit, a little pink robe and heels.

Born Ready continued studying the chessboard in front of him. No pieces had been moved. Everything was still on the starting squares. "Before a war, you gotta figure all the possible outcomes. Some moves can't be taken back, so you gotta prepare for everything."

"Just don't let it consume you. I don't like when you think too much. You get quiet and don't talk to me."

180

"That's because I need to make the right moves. Somebody killed my brotha. I only got a couple options. B-Real, Pop Somethin', and Grind Squad."

"Him and Pop had problems while they was locked up. I think it's him. B-Real scared of yo' brotha. I know he wouldn't be able to come around you without actin' funny, but Pop Somethin' is a killa. I think that nigga could kill his momma and not feel bad about it."

"Yeah. I feel the same way, but I can't prove it, and I need some type of proof before I bring it to this nigga. I can't come at him half-cocked. Plus, Grind Squad is still out there. I can't put nothin' past them."

"So, what you gon' do?"

"The only thing I can do."

"And that is?"

Born Ready looked up from the chessboard and smiled at his big, beautiful woman. "Don't worry, baby. I'm two steps ahead of er'body. It's all gon' work out in time."

Sasha smiled and licked her lips. "I like when you be mysterious. That shit be makin' me wanna do shit to you."

"Don't let me get in the way of you gettin' what you want."

Sasha got up and stood in front of Born Ready doing a sexy shimmy-dance. The way too small bathrobe came off, revealing her curvy, full-figured body, breasts as big as watermelons, a slight pudge on her stomach, wide hips, and thick thighs. She continued dancing for Born Ready before sitting on his lap and giving him a lap dance.

After a few minutes of grinding, she spun around and began undressing him. When he was naked, she knelt between his legs and took his dick in her mouth. She made love to it, kissing, licking, and sucking him.

Sasha's lips was exactly what Born Ready needed to clear his mind of death and murder. A few minutes later he erupted in her mouth. Sasha stared up at him as she swallowed every drop.

When she seen he was still hard, she stood up, spun around, and grabbed her ankles. Born Ready stood behind her, digging his stick into her sugary walls. He whaled away at her pussy from the back. When she got tired of standing and holding her ankles, she bent over the couch. Born Ready got behind her and continued to assault her pussy. Sasha went wild from the pounding her man was putting down. A few minutes later Born Ready's body locked.

***

B-Real loved his red Maybach like he had created it with his own hands. White leather seats, an infotainment screen and controller, curtains in the windows, climate-controlled seats, and enough room to fold a nigga up on the floor like Buck Wild had done to Ken-Ken.

"The streets is ours, dawg. Profits is up. My pockets is up. My whip game is up. I feel like life is some good-ass pussy, and I'm fuckin' the shit out that bitch!" B-Real laughed, slapping the dashboard.

Born Ready sat in the passenger seat wearing a sly grin. "Life is about winnin', mane. If you ain't winnin', you ain't livin'."

"Oh, Pop. I just got that paperwork back on the Batmobile. And I got you and yo' bitches other driver's license. Names clean. No records. Y'all good as new, my nigga," B-Real said, going in the console and giving Pop Somethin' all the information.

"Quinton Rose? Rodney Rollins? Cris Livingston?" Pop questioned. "You coulda gave me at least one name that sounded Jamaican or African to fit my look."

"Chill, Q. You good," Born Ready laughed. "All Qs ain't pretty boys. I did a bid with a nigga name Q that was savage. Animal, brah. Niggas didn't want none."

A Gangster's Code 2

"I ain't trippin' on that. My name ring enough bells. Plus, this what we needed to plant our roots in a new spot. I think I'm 'bout ready to move on."

Pop Somethin's admission that he wanted to leave Atlanta sucked all the air out of the car like a vacuum. "You wanna leave?" B-Real asked, looking at Pop through the rearview mirror like he was crazy. "The streets is ours. We fuckin' up big bags. Grind Squad outta the way. The takeover is real. We 'bout to be millionaires. And you wanna walk away?"

"Pop, I thought we talked about this," Born Ready said. "Five more months to get a mil. Talk to me, my nigga. Why now?"

"The bodies pilin' up. I think it's only a matter of time before the feds get in it because of those fags gettin' knocked off. They gon' look into who Marks an' 'em was fuckin' wit'. I don't wanna be in town when that happens. Plus, Grind Squad ain't gone. They layin' low. You know it too, Born Ready. You too smart to be fooled by they fall back. Don't nobody walk away from they bag, especially if you had to fight to get it."

The Maybach grew quiet as Pop's words marinated. "You America's nightmare, Pop," Born Ready chuckled. "Smart, instinctive, war ready. Yeah, I thought about D.D. gettin' away and shuttin' they shit down. No way I would walk away without fightin' over my shit. I know he gon' hit back, and ain't nothin' we can do but wait. They off the grid. Gotta see his next move and then react. And that's why I need you wit' me, Pop. I need you wit' me when we make the counter move."

"If I didn't think the feds was gon' get involved, I would stay. Atlanta been good to me, but I'm the kinda nigga that move on vibes, how I feel, and what my gut tell me. And it's time for me to go."

"We got a team, Pop. We got soldiers. If you wanna get security like the president, just say it," B-Real said.

"You missin' what we talkin' 'bout," Born Ready cut in. "This ain't about security. He thinkin' 'bout liberty. Freedom."

The Maybach grew quiet again.

"Lemme ask you niggas somethin'," Born Ready spoke up. "I spoke to Marks the night he died, and he told me some shit that fucked me up. He was lookin' into who killed–"

Breaking glass and projectiles slamming into the luxury car cut off the conversation, and they flinched and ducked for cover. A dark-colored SUV had pulled along the driver's side of the Maybach. People hung out of the front and rear passenger windows, firing automatic weapons. B-Real's body jerked as 9mm bullets tore into him.

Instead of trying to hide, Pop Somethin' pulled the door lever and dove from the Maybach. The luxury car traveled at twenty-five miles an hour. After a few rolls, Pop Somethin' stood, the 50-caliber Desert Eagle jumping into his hand like a magnet was in his palm. The Maybach crashed as the Dodge Durango sped away. Pop Somethin' emptied the Desert Eagle clip at the fleeing truck. After reloading, he ran to the Maybach to check on the S.O.D. leaders. B-Real was slumped against the steering wheel, blood leaking from his body. Born Ready lay on the floor of the passenger seat, curled in a ball.

"Born Ready, you good?" Pop called.

The last living S.O.D. leader moved slowly. "Yeah." When he got up, he looked at B-Real. "Damn. They fucked him up. That was Grind Squad. You know what this mean, right?"

Chapter 19

Seeing Shanice's face on the phone screen sent a flash of excitement through Queenie's body. They hadn't talked since she left Atlanta. There was so much to talk about.

"Hey," Queenie said evenly, keeping her feelings in check.

"Hey," Shanice responded, her voice barely above a whisper. "I'm sorry I didn't talk to you before I left. I just wanted to call and let you know it wasn't like that. For everything to happen how it did, I was pissed when he came at me like that."

"I understood, Shanice. Trust me. Nothin' worked out the way we expected. I'm sorry I didn't tell you about C-Note, but that was for you and Pop to work out. I didn't want to get in that. That was a family situation."

"I know. I probably would've done the same thing if I was in your shoes."

The pause in the conversation was noticeable, like both women were waiting for the other to make the next move. Queenie spoke up. "How you been? I've been thinkin' 'bout you a lot."

Shanice's voice became a whisper again. "I lost the baby."

The news stunned Queenie. "What? When? You okay?"

"As soon as I left the house, while I was in the airport. I stayed in Atlanta for a week at the hospital."

"Why didn't you call me? I would've come."

"Because I was mad at him. I still am. He took everything from me. How can you hurt somebody you supposed to love like that? He took my baby and my man. I hate him. I hope he has bad luck for the rest of his life."

"Shanice, don't say that, girl. You don't mean it. You just hurtin'."

"I am hurt. And I mean every word. He took my family. I wish I could hurt him myself. I want him to know how I feel."

"Damn, Shanice. I'm sorry for everything. I ain't gon' even say I know how you feel, 'cause I don't, but as a woman and somebody who cares about you, I feel yo' pain. And if I can do anything to help you, just let me know. I got you."

"Can you be my friend again?" Shanice asked timidly.

"I'ma always be that. I told you I'll always be here."

"You the best thing that's happened to me in a long time. Not talking to you was torture. I'm so lonely in Fort Worth. I'm thinking of moving back to Houston to be around family. The only reason I moved here was for Nitty."

"That might not be a bad idea. It might do you good to be around loved ones, especially after everything you been through. You need some TLC. Have you told anyone what happened?"

"Yeah. I talked to my mom and cousin. I told them I lost the baby and C-Note died. I didn't tell them he did it. Momma want me to come help her out. After all them people died in the house, she moved. We grew up in that house, so it was hard to leave."

"Damn. I'm sorry to hear that. We about to move, too. Atlanta is heatin' up."

Shanice laughed. "That's what my cousin do. Everywhere he go, he set it on fire. You really wanna live like that?"

"Yeah. For now. I wish you could've stayed with us. I miss you so much."

"I don't even want to think about that. I just want you. If you ever get tired of the drama, you can always come home."

The front door opening interrupted their conversation. Pop Somethin' and Born Ready walked in wearing serious looks. "Let me call you back," Queenie said, ending the call. "You good, baby? What happened?"

"Grind Squad hit back. B-Real dead."

A Gangster's Code 2

Queenie's face turned as serious as Pop's, murder in her eyes. "Where them niggas at? What you want me to do?"

"We gotta put our feelers out and see what we catch. I need you and Princess to hit them clubs and see what niggas sayin'. We gotta find a way to get to these niggas."

"What niggas?" Princess asked, walking into the living room.

"Grind Squad," Queenie answered. "They hit Pop an' 'em and killed B-Real. We gotta get out there and see what niggas is sayin'. Somebody know somethin'. We gotta find out who."

"I like her," Born Ready said, eyeing Queenie.

"Shouldn't we just leave, Pop?" Princess asked. "We talked about this the other night. Let's leave wit' what we got so we won't leave wit' nothin'."

"It's bigger than that. This ain't no cartel. These niggas took a shot at me. I wanna shoot back, show these niggas the G on my gangsta bigger than all theirs."

"C'mon, Pop. This ain't about gettin' a lick back. We gotta be smart, baby. Right now we got more than we came with. Let's just go," Princess pleaded.

"You doin' exactly what you s'posed to, baby. And you right. We should leave. And we will. But not right now. I wanna hit these niggas hard before we leave. Show these niggas how real killas move."

***

The action at Kitty's was stagnant. Ever since Grind Squad left town, the money slowed. Now that S.O.D. was on high alert, the strippers were lucky to make a hundred dollars a night. A few regulars with nine-to-fives and small-time hustlers were spread out in the club. Tips were hard to get when the big dogs didn't come out, so Queenie and Princess sat at the bar, nursing watery drinks. Watching. Waiting. Lurking.

Three days had passed since the hit. S.O.D. was off the street. Everybody had feelers out, trying to get a piece of information that would give them an edge.

A boisterous laugh at the door got the twins' attention. The owner of the laugh wasn't well known in Atlanta, but no one could tell him that. In Ranell's mind, he was bigger than all the stars in Atlanta. He went from bred in the slums to partying with ballers. He was living the life every nigga in the hood wanted, so he rocked that shit on his sleeves like a Gucci G. He was tall and broad with dark brown skin and bright eyes that only seen show lights. He had shoulder-length dreads, a face clean shaven except for a pencil-thin mustache. Designer brands covered him from jacket to shoes. The two niggas with him looked plain standing next to a light that shined as bright as Ranell's.

"Yeah, hos! Turn up! Grind Squad in the muthafuckin' buildin'!"

Queenie and Princess looked to each other at the same time, eyes wide like they were Megabucks winners. The twins watched the crew of three move through the almost empty club like they were twenty deep. They went directly to the bar, standing a few feet from the sisters.

"Lemme get three bottles of Vanilla CÎROC and two bottles of Aces," Ranell ordered, pulling a knot of cash as big as the Bible from his pocket.

One of the ordinary niggas next to Ranell noticed the sisters. "Damn! Y'all twins?" he asked, ogling them like they were magical creatures.

Princess's eyes got smaller than a snake's as she chose her prey. "Grind Squad in the buildin', huh? 'Bout time some niggas wit' clout showed up. Got all these funny-lookin', broke niggas in here trynna catch a date wit' a work check."

"I get mo' money in six months than what's in them niggas' safe. I'm Ranell. Y'all come fuck wit' us tonight. These my niggas, Trey-Five-Seven and Varen."

The twins showered Ranell with attention, lap dances, and body rubs. An hour later he was sandwiched between them. Queenie rubbed his chest. Princess's hand was on his thigh. "So, where y'all niggas been at? Had bitches strugglin' to buy a new bag. I heard Grind Squad was done after Sid got killed."

Encouraged by the liquor and sexy atmosphere created by the seducers, Ranell's mouth became a waterfall. "Nah, we ain't lettin' that bitch-ass shit fold us. D.D. and the rest us niggas too strong to fold up. We ain't just in Atlanta. We all over. Philly. New York. Chicago. Detroit. We finna flood this bitch and take over. S.O.D. local. They ain't got enough manpower to face us."

"Damn, daddy! I didn't know y'all was nationwide," Queenie said, her eyes wide in amazement. "I know once y'all press, y'all gon' take over. I ain't no gold digger, but I don't wanna fuck no broke niggas. Me and my sister can be by yo' side when y'all take over."

Princess grabbed his earlobe between her lips and bit down lightly. "And we the kinda sisters that kiss each other when ain't nobody lookin'."

Ranell's eyes got wide as a full moon. "Put ch'all numba in my phone. Matter fact, I need to see this kissin' before I close my eyes. If y'all ain't got no rules or curfews, come fuck wit' me. My Aviator outside."

"What about yo' niggas?" Princess asked.

"Them niggas came together. I'm solo-dolo. Got enough room for a party in my Lincoln truck.

***

J-Blunt

The Batmobile carved through the Atlanta streets like a predator seeking prey. Zero to 62 miles an hour in 3.6 seconds and steering that made Pop's hands feel like they were part of the car. Nothing on the road seemed powerful enough to stand in the machine's path. Violence emanated from the twin turbo-charged V-8 engine when it pulled to a stop behind the black Lincoln Aviator waiting at the red light. The light turned green as action in the truck began.

At the next stop light, the Lambo doors lifted and the killas stepped out. Pop opened the passenger door. Queenie held a gun on Ranell. The look on his face reflected the deep pile of dog shit he'd stepped in. Pop leaned in to kiss Queenie. "Good shit, baby. Y'all go to the Batmobile. We got it from here."

"See if he jack for y'all how he was jackin' for us. Grind Squad bigger than we think, baby. S.O.D. is the little brother."

When Queenie got out of the truck, Pop took her place. Born Ready replaced Princess in the back seat. Neither goon showed a weapon, but Ranell still felt threatened. Pop looked like a boogey man in the passenger seat, muscles bulging from the snug black t-shirt. The beard and dreads hid most of his face, so Ranell wasn't sure what he looked like.

"Drive, nigga!" Born Ready barked after the light changed.

"Uh, wh-where we goin'?" Ranell stuttered.

"Take us to D.D. We got a message for him."

"I-I d-don't know where he at."

Pop Somethin' pulled a six-inch switchblade from his pocket.

"Lie to me again, Ranell, and he gon' fuck you up." Born Ready warned. "Take us to yo' boss."

"I-I'm for real. I. *Ah!*"

Pop's hand was a blur. Before Ranell knew he was stabbed, Pop Somethin's hand was already resting at his side again. Ranell kept a hand on his ribs, trying to stop the blood.

"You a hard-headed-ass nigga, ain't chu?" Born Ready taunted. "Yo' life on the line, kid. Who it gon' be? You or some nigga you work for?"

"I ain't plugged all the way in. I'm just. *Ah!*" Ranell grabbed his chest after the knife left his pectoral.

"You see he gettin' higher wit' that steel thang. Say somethin', nigga. Save yo'self."

"All I know is where his brother's at. D.D. still in Chicago."

"There you go, Ranell. Betta save yo' ass, boy. Tell me 'bout this brotha while you drive over there."

The house wasn't a house, but a small four-unit apartment building that had been converted into a mini-mansion. Queenie and Princess climbed from the Lambo like they were trying to catch a date in heels, leggings, and spaghetti tops. After ringing the bell, the door was opened. A short, dark-skinned nigga with gold-rimmed glasses answered. When he seen the women, he took a step back to check them out. "What up wit' ch'all? Who y'all here for?"

Princess spoke up. "Ranell told us to meet him over here. He here yet?"

"Ranell?" he questioned. Then a light went on in his mind. "Oh, yeah. Ranell. Yeah, yeah. He did call and say y'all was comin'. Damn, y'all bad. Come in. We in the back. Who is y'all? I'm Lib."

"I'm Queenie."

"I'm Princess," the sisters said as they stepped into the apartment building. It had thick, blue-carpeted floors, and all the doors were open like it was a house with four rooms instead of a four-unit apartment building. The apartment/room in back turned out to be a studio. Two niggas were in the booth recording, and one was at the controls. When Lib walked in, all eyes flocked to his guests. Queenie and Princess waved as they went to sit on a couch.

"Who dat?" the controller asked. He was chubby and light-skinned with a short, nappy afro.

"Queenie and Princess. Ranell sent them. He on his way."

The controller looked at the women. "I'm Geo. Y'all drink or smoke?"

Queenie eyed the ounce of lime green on the table. "We smoke."

Conversation flowed as they smoked. When the rappers finished recording, they came out to meet the guests. When the men learned they were strippers, a good time was had by all, and the Grind Squad members forgot about Ranell. Nobody noticed Queenie take her phone to the bathroom. After a few text messages, she rejoined the party.

"Damn. Here go Ranell fool ass," Lib said, reading a text. Anxious to get back to the stripping twin sisters, he went to unlock the door without looking outside.

The Desert Eagle came flying in, breaking his jaw. Lib fell to the floor, clutching his mangled face. Pop Somethin' stood over him, the hand cannon pointing at Lib like a sword. "Get up, nigga! Don't say shit. Walk to the studio."

Ranell led the way to the back apartment like a cow being led to the slaughter. As soon as he stepped into the room, the Desert Eagle barked. A chunk of Lib's skull exploded, blood and brains staining the carpet where the body fell. Geo and the rappers froze, their eyes and mouths wide with terror.

Queenie and Princess stood to dress.

"We ain't got time to play games, niggas. Where D.D. at?" Born Ready asked, waving a Tech-9.

One of the rappers took the first try. "We ain't heard from D.D. in a minute, nigga"

Pop-pop-pop-pop! The Tech-9 sounded as four bullets took his voice box.

A Gangster's Code 2

"Where D.D.?" Born Ready asked again, waving the murder weapon.

The remaining rapper and Geo looked at each other, wondering who would be the first to snitch. Their indecision made the Tech spit again. Two bullets to the face cost the rapper his life.

"You the last man standin'. Yo' name Geo, right? You D.D. brotha? I know you know where he at. You let yo' niggas die for nothin'," Born Ready said.

Surprise showed on the chubby, light-skinned man's face. "Uh. He. He at the compound. Y'all won't be able to get in. We heavy over there."

"Where the compound at?" Pop Somethin' asked.

The snitch hesitated. Born Ready waved the Tech.

After a five-minute confession, they learned the compound was a subdivision on Druid Hill Road. It was Grind Squad headquarters in Atlanta. The house was a stronghold and usually kept about ten people inside. Since Grind Squad was getting ready to press S.O.D., 20 to 25 people were inside.

After getting what they needed, Born Ready executed the final Grind Squad member before leaving the house.

J-Blunt

Chapter 20

Born Ready fumed as he paced the living room, walking from the front door to the kitchen so many times he created a trail in the carpet. The phone in his hand was the cause of the contempt. S.O.D. was moving on. G-Slim was on the other end of the line delivering the news.

"We ain't finna fuck wit' chu like dat, nigga. You fucked wit' B-Real. Dat nigga dead. You ain't from 'round here, brah. We ain't finna follow you."

"C'mon, G-Slim. I put in work for S.O.D. Y'all gon' put me on my ass after all that shit I did?"

"Yeah, nigga. You an outsider. Only reason we fucked wit' chu was 'cause B-Real vouched for you. We don't let new niggas in. We talked enough. S.O.D. movin' on. Do you."

Born Ready slipped the phone in his pocket and fell onto the couch.

"You knew that was gon' happen," Pop spoke up.

"Yeah, I know. I just didn't want it to be over like this. Shit was sweet as fuck. Damn, I was almost a millionaire," Born Ready sighed regrettably.

"I'm leavin' wit' almost half a ticket. I ain't got no complaints."

"Yeah, when you put it like that, it don't sound bad. At least we leavin' wit' somethin'. Fuck it. Sun don't shine forever. I'm goin' back to Houston. Where you goin'?"

"We thinkin' 'bout Florida. See some beaches an' shit. Try to make a few moves before I go back to the island. I still ain't hit my goal."

"And what's that? What island you talkin' 'bout?"

Pop smiled. "The only one that matter. Jamaica. I was trynna check a mil and go home. Open up a hotel and lay back and enjoy the good life."

Born Ready looked impressed. "That don't sound bad, nigga. What them Jamaican bitches like? They cut off niggas' dicks if they get caught cheatin'?"

"I don't think they no different than the females here. Fuck over the wrong one and that's yo' ass."

"Jamaica got them old African roots," Born Ready laughed. "Warrior women tribes an' shit. Sacrificing niggas to the gods."

"Fool-ass nigga!" Pop laughed. "What bullshit-ass white-washed history book you read that in?"

"I'm just fuckin' wit' chu, dawg," Born Ready said, standing. "I gotta get to the crib and pack. We on the first thang smoking to H-Town."

Pop stood to walk his comrade to the door. "I'ma move a li'l faster than you. We out this bitch right now. That body count up there. The sooner we out, the better."

After a handshake and hug, Born Ready stepped outside. The vibrating of his phone stopped him. He didn't know the number, so he answered on speaker. "What up?"

"This Born Ready, right?"

The voice stopped the goon in his tracks. When Pop seen the reaction, he moved closer to the phone. Based on Born Ready's reaction, Pop knew whoever was on the phone was important.

"Yeah, this Born Ready. Who dis?"

"We never officially met, but this D.D. The one you missed."

Born Ready and Pop's eyes met. Neither spoke.

D.D. continued. "So, I guess you know who I am, right? You got that otha nigga wit' chu? Pop Somethin'?"

"I hear you," Pop spoke up.

"You niggas almost pulled it off. I gotta hand it to y'all. If we was any other organization, y'all woulda beat us. Took me longer than expected to get this number. But now that I got ch'all attention, lemme say this. We comin' for you niggas. And I know 'bout them twin bitches, too, Pop Somethin'. I got prices on all y'all heads. Hunnit Gs a pop. Killas out here lurkin'."

"Y'all can have this shit back. I got what I came for," Born Ready said. "I'ma be gone by the mornin'. But since we talkin', tell me what you did wit' my brotha body so I can take him home."

"You gotta ask the nigga standin' next to you. He was the last one seen wit' 'im. They left Kitty's together the night he came up missin'. Look him in the eyes and tell me what you see."

Pop Somethin's eyes were dark and hard as steel, and they also promised violence to a degree the average man wouldn't understand. Born Ready got the confirmation he needed. He knew it all along. He just needed proof and opportunity. They had fallen into his lap at the same time. Pop Somethin' wasn't strapped, but he was too close for Born Ready to pull his pistol and get a shot off. The master chess player knew Pop was just as dangerous without a gun if he could lay a hand on a nigga.

"What car you want the money in?" Queenie asked, walking outside with a duffel bag with $200,000 in it.

Pop took his eyes off Born Ready for a split second. Queenie didn't realize what was happening until Born Ready grabbed her, using her as a shield as he pulled the 9mm Smith and Wesson from his waist.

"Don't flex, bitch! And you betta not move, Pop!" Born Ready said, backing away from the porch and making sure to keep Queenie between him and Pop Somethin'.

The dreadlocked grim reaper tried to think of something that would give him an advantage. He wasn't armed, and Born Ready had a gun, his girl, and his money. And he didn't' have much time to think because as soon as Born Ready created enough space, he took aim at Pop Somethin'.

Pop-pop-pop-pop-pop-pop-pop!

J-Blunt

The big man anticipated the move, diving into the house as the bullets tore into the front door. Pop was on his feet in the blink of an eye, moving for the AR-l5 under the couch. After grabbing the chopper, he ran outside. Born Ready was in the passenger seat of the green Aston Martin. Queenie drove, the Smith and Wesson to her head.

To Be Continued...
A Gangsta's Code 3
Coming Soon

Submission Guideline.

Submit the first three chapters of your completed manuscript to ldpsubmissions@gmail.com, subject line: Your book's title. The manuscript must be in a .doc file and sent as an attachment. Document should be in Times New Roman, double spaced and in size 12 font. Also, provide your synopsis and full contact information. If sending multiple submissions, they must each be in a separate email.

Have a story but no way to send it electronically? You can still submit to LDP/Ca$h Presents. Send in the first three chapters, written or typed, of your completed manuscript to:

LDP: Submissions Dept
Po Box 870494
Mesquite, Tx 75187

DO NOT send original manuscript. Must be a duplicate.

Provide your synopsis and a cover letter containing your full contact information.

Thanks for considering LDP and Ca$h Presents.

Coming Soon from Lock Down Publications/Ca$h Presents

BOW DOWN TO MY GANGSTA

By **Ca$h**

TORN BETWEEN TWO

By **Coffee**

BLOOD STAINS OF A SHOTTA **III**

By **Jamaica**

STEADY MOBBIN II

By **Marcellus Allen**

BLOOD OF A BOSS **V**

By **Askari**

LOYAL TO THE GAME **IV**

By **T.J. & Jelissa**

A DOPEBOY'S PRAYER **II**

By **Eddie "Wolf" Lee**

IF LOVING YOU IS WRONG... **III**

LOVE ME EVEN WHEN IT HURTS

By **Jelissa**

TRUE SAVAGE **V**

By **Chris Green**

TRAPHOUSE KING **III**

By **Hood Rich**

BLAST FOR ME **III**

ROTTEN TO THE CORE **II**

By **Ghost**

ADDICTIED TO THE DRAMA **III**

By **Jamila Mathis**

A Gangster's Code 2

LIPSTICK KILLAH **III**

CRIME OF PASSION **II**

By **Mimi**

WHAT BAD BITCHES DO **III**

By **Aryanna**

THE COST OF LOYALTY **II**

By **Kweli**

SHE FELL IN LOVE WITH A REAL ONE **II**

By **Tamara Butler**

LOVE SHOULDN'T HURT **III**

By **Meesha**

CORRUPTED BY A GANGSTA **III**

By **Destiny Skai**

A GANGSTER'S CODE III

By **J-Blunt**

KING OF NEW YORK II

By **T.J. Edwards**

CUM FOR ME **IV**

By **Ca$h & Company**

Available Now

RESTRAINING ORDER **I & II**

By **CA$H & Coffee**

LOVE KNOWS NO BOUNDARIES **I II & III**

By **Coffee**

RAISED AS A GOON I, II, III & IV

BRED BY THE SLUMS I, II, III

J-Blunt

BLAST FOR ME I & II
ROTTEN TO THE CORE
By **Ghost**
LAY IT DOWN **I & II**
LAST OF A DYING BREED
BLOOD STAINS OF A SHOTTA I & II
By **Jamaica**
LOYAL TO THE GAME
LOYAL TO THE GAME II
LOYAL TO THE GAME III
By **TJ & Jelissa**
BLOODY COMMAS I & II
SKI MASK CARTEL I II & III
KING OF NEW YORK
By **T.J. Edwards**
IF LOVING HIM IS WRONG…I & II
By **Jelissa**
WHEN THE STREETS CLAP BACK I & II III
By **Jibril Williams**
A DISTINGUISHED THUG STOLE MY HEART I II & III
LOVE SHOULDN'T HURT I II
By **Meesha**
A GANGSTER'S CODE I & II
By J-Blunt
PUSH IT TO THE LIMIT
By **Bre' Hayes**
BLOOD OF A BOSS **I, II, III & IV**
By **Askari**

202

A Gangster's Code 2

THE STREETS BLEED MURDER **I, II & III**

THE HEART OF A GANGSTA I II& III

By **Jerry Jackson**

CUM FOR ME

CUM FOR ME 2

CUM FOR ME 3

An **LDP Erotica Collaboration**

BRIDE OF A HUSTLA **I II & II**

THE FETTI GIRLS **I, II& III**

CORRUPTED BY A GANGSTA I & II

By **Destiny Skai**

WHEN A GOOD GIRL GOES BAD

By **Adrienne**

A GANGSTER'S REVENGE **I II III & IV**

THE BOSS MAN'S DAUGHTERS

THE BOSS MAN'S DAUGHTERS II

THE BOSSMAN'S DAUGHTERS III

THE BOSSMAN'S DAUGHTERS IV

THE BOSS MAN'S DAUGHTERS **V**

A SAVAGE LOVE **I & II**

BAE BELONGS TO ME

A HUSTLER'S DECEIT I, II

WHAT BAD BITCHES DO I, II

By **Aryanna**

A KINGPIN'S AMBITON

A KINGPIN'S AMBITION **II**

I MURDER FOR THE DOUGH

By **Ambitious**

TRUE SAVAGE

TRUE SAVAGE II

TRUE SAVAGE **III**

TRUE SAVAGE **IV**

By **Chris Green**

A DOPEBOY'S PRAYER

By **Eddie "Wolf" Lee**

THE KING CARTEL **I, II & III**

By **Frank Gresham**

THESE NIGGAS AIN'T LOYAL **I, II & III**

By **Nikki Tee**

GANGSTA SHYT **I II &III**

By **CATO**

THE ULTIMATE BETRAYAL

By **Phoenix**

BOSS'N UP **I , II & III**

By **Royal Nicole**

I LOVE YOU TO DEATH

By Destiny J

I RIDE FOR MY HITTA

I STILL RIDE FOR MY HITTA

By **Misty Holt**

LOVE & CHASIN' PAPER

By **Qay Crockett**

TO DIE IN VAIN

By **ASAD**

BROOKLYN HUSTLAZ

By **Boogsy Morina**

A Gangster's Code 2

BROOKLYN ON LOCK I & II

By **Sonovia**

GANGSTA CITY

By **Teddy Duke**

A DRUG KING AND HIS DIAMOND I & II

A DOPEMAN'S RICHES

By Nicole Goosby

TRAPHOUSE KING I & II

By **Hood Rich**

LIPSTICK KILLAH **I, II**

CRIME OF PASSION

By **Mimi**

STEADY MOBBN'

By **Marcellus Allen**

BOOKS BY LDP'S CEO, CA$H

TRUST IN NO MAN

TRUST IN NO MAN 2

TRUST IN NO MAN 3

BONDED BY BLOOD

SHORTY GOT A THUG

THUGS CRY

THUGS CRY 2

THUGS CRY 3

TRUST NO BITCH

TRUST NO BITCH 2

TRUST NO BITCH 3

TIL MY CASKET DROPS

RESTRAINING ORDER

RESTRAINING ORDER 2

IN LOVE WITH A CONVICT

Coming Soon

BONDED BY BLOOD 2

BOW DOWN TO MY GANGSTA

A Gangster's Code 2

www.ingramcontent.com/pod-product-compliance
Lightning Source LLC
Chambersburg PA
CBHW070011260626
47159CB00005B/1751